It's Cindy's worst nightmare....

"I just got a call from Brad Tow

Cindy felt her stomach tens
of her neck prickled as though
over her. Anything to do with
be bad news. What could he
Oaks?

Ben exhaled slowly and sat
Cindy's eyes. "The problem ha

Cindy went rigid. She narrowed her eyes, feeling her heart sink. "What could Brad possibly have on Champion?" she demanded. "Clay Townsend sold his interest in Champion to your father years ago."

Ben rose and walked across the room, stopping near a wall Cindy had covered with photos of racehorses. Ben picked up a glass statue of Secretariat and turned it over and over, avoiding Cindy's eyes. She felt herself becoming more tense as Ben's silence stretched on for several seconds. Finally he replaced the figurine and looked up at her, his dark eyes troubled.

"Brad says he has papers that show the sale of Champion to the al-Rihanis was never completed," he said. "According to Brad, Townsend Acres still owns the stallion, and they want him back."

Collect all the books in the Thoroughbred series

Collect all the books in the Ashleigh series

coming soon*

THOROUGHBRED

CINDY'S LAST HOPE

CREATED BY

JOANNA CAMPBELL

WRITTEN BY

MARY ANDERSON

HarperEntertainment

An Imprint of HarperCollinsPublishers

HarperEntertainment

An Imprint of HarperCollins*Publishers*

10 East 53rd Street, New York, NY 10022-5299

This is a work of fiction. The characters, incidents, and dialogues are products of the author's imagination and are not to be construed as real. Any resemblance to actual events or persons, living or dead, is entirely coincidental.

 Produced by 17th Street Productions, an Alloy Online, Inc., company

HarperCollins books are available at special quantity discounts for bulk purchases for sales promotions, premiums, or fund-raising. For information please call or write: Special Markets Department, HarperCollins Publishers Inc., 10 East 53rd Street, New York, NY 10022-5299. Telephone: (212) 207-7528. Fax: (212) 207-7222.

ISBN 0-06-009046-4

HarperCollins®, ® , and HarperEntertainment™ are trademarks of HarperCollins Publishers Inc.

Cover art © 2002 by 17th Street Productions, an Alloy Online, Inc., company

First printing: August 2002

Printed in the United States of America

Visit HarperEntertainment on the World Wide Web at www.harpercollins.com

❖ 10 9 8 7 6 5 4 3 2 1

1

"Just look at him, Ben," Cindy McLean said, gazing across the pasture at Wonder's Champion. "Have you ever seen such a beautiful creature?" She rested her forearms on the top rail of the paddock fence, admiring the chestnut stallion who stood in the middle of the grassy enclosure. When tall, dark-haired Ben didn't respond, Cindy looked up at him—and immediately felt a blush creep up her cheeks. Ben al-Rihani was gazing down at her, a half smile tugging at the corners of his mouth.

"Why are you staring at me?" Cindy demanded, swiping at a few stray wisps of blond hair and tucking the short strands behind her ear.

"Quite honestly," Ben said, his smile getting a little wider, "I *have* seen one other creature as kind to the eyes as your beautiful Champion out there." He nodded toward the stallion, but his attention stayed on Cindy. "You look radiant right now. If I had known that bringing that horse home from Dubai would put such a light in your eyes, I would have acted much sooner."

Cindy felt her face grow even warmer, and she was sure her cheeks were bright pink. She quickly looked away from Ben, focusing on Champion again. "He's home now," she said. "That's what's important."

Champion lowered his elegant nose to sniff at the thick bluegrass underfoot. He nipped at the grass, then suddenly dropped to his knees and flopped sideways to enjoy a brisk roll. His graceful legs thrashed the air as he rubbed his back in the soft grass. Then, with a joyful snort, he lunged to his feet and shook himself thoroughly.

Cindy burst into laughter at the eighteen-year-old stallion's undignified behavior. "He's acting like a colt," she exclaimed. As if he could understand her, Champion raised his head, once again assuming the regal pose of a mature Thoroughbred stallion. He cast a disdainful glance in their direction, then turned his back to Ben and Cindy. Ambling across the paddock, he grazed steadily as he walked away.

"I think you embarrassed him," Ben said with a soft chuckle.

"He shouldn't act so silly if he doesn't want to be laughed at," Cindy said, her attention still fixed on Champion. To her, the stallion looked perfectly content as he wandered around the large pasture.

Tall Oaks Farm, the Thoroughbred breeding and training facility Ben owned, was the perfect home for Champion. The stallion had been born and raised at another Kentucky horse farm, Whitebrook, where Cindy's adoptive father, Ian McLean, was the head trainer. But as a three-year-old, after winning the prestigious Triple Crown, Champion had been sold to the al-Rihanis. For more than a dozen years the stallion had lived in the Arabian desert at a Thoroughbred farm owned by Ben's father, Sheik Habib al-Rihani.

Cindy had traveled to Dubai with Champion but returned to the Unites States after working for the al-Rihanis for a year. When she had left the stallion in the United Arab Emirates so many years before, the stallion had seemed at peace in his ancestral home. But now, back in the place where he had spent his first three years, the long-retired racehorse seemed even more content.

"Thank you for bringing him home," Cindy said, daring to look up at Ben again.

His smile was sincere and friendly, not at all trying to tease her into another blushing episode. "He belongs here," Ben said. "Just like you do."

"I love working at Tall Oaks," Cindy agreed, looking around at the large, well-built barns and the sprawling fields that stretched as far as she could see.

"I meant in Kentucky," Ben corrected her. "I remember the year you spent at my father's stable. The change was such a struggle for you. You worked so hard to fit in there. I know it was a difficult time."

Cindy grimaced at the memory. "It wasn't easy," she admitted. "But I learned a lot during that year, and it helped make me tougher."

"You don't look so tough," Ben said, looking down at petite Cindy.

"Tell that to the New York jockeys I spent twelve years racing against," Cindy retorted, standing as tall as she could. "Or the horses I rode. They'll tell you I don't put up with any nonsense."

Ben raised his eyebrows in mock surprise. "Talking horses? We have no such animals in the United Arab Emirates. This must be something only American horses can do."

Cindy groaned. "Never mind," she said, rolling her eyes as Ben laughed at his own joke.

"Speaking of putting up with nonsense from horses," Ben said, suddenly serious, "didn't you say we have a new jockey coming to give Gratis a tryout?"

Cindy looked at her watch and gasped. "Yes," she said. "He should have been here a few minutes ago. We'd better get over to the track."

As Tall Oaks' farm manager, Cindy was responsible for overseeing all the activities involving the Thoroughbreds. Finding a jockey for Gratis, the farm's Kentucky Derby entry, was her biggest challenge since taking the job.

Cindy and Ben turned away from Champion and hurried toward the barns and Tall Oaks' practice track. As they came around the corner of one of the farm's large barns, Cindy saw a groom leading a tall bay colt toward the track. She winced as the colt swung his head at the groom, his teeth bared.

"Look out!" she yelled. But before the man could react, Gratis chomped into his arm. The handler let out a howl of pain. Cindy ran toward the pair as fast as she could.

The groom, a tall, thin, middle-aged man who had only been at the farm for a few days, shoved Gratis's lead line into Cindy's hands. "That's it!" he said, taking several steps away from Gratis. "That horse has tried to kick me and run me over, and now he's trying to eat me! I quit!" He turned and strode away, rubbing his arm as he left.

Cindy watched in dismay as the groom stormed off. Ben reached her side and looked from their former employee to Gratis, then to Cindy. "Another one?" he asked in a mild voice.

"That's three grooms in two weeks," Cindy said, narrowing her eyes as she glared at Gratis. The colt lifted his nose in the air and curled his lip. "And look at him," she said in disgust. "He looks like he's laughing his tail off about it." A car door slammed, and she watched the angry groom speed down the long driveway and away from Tall Oaks. "I don't even remember that groom's name," she said.

"It'll be in his employment file," Ben told her. "I'll make sure he gets his pay."

"You'd better add a little for hazardous duty," Cindy said. She frowned at Gratis, but the colt looked completely remorseless. She gave Gratis's lead line a firm tug. The colt angled his head and gave her a curious look. "You are a monster," she told him, trying to keep the fondness she felt for the colt out of her voice. Gratis dropped his nose and followed Cindy calmly as she walked toward the track.

A small man was leaning against the rail surrounding the practice track, a riding crop stuffed in the back pocket of his jeans, a helmet dangling from his fingertips. He turned as Cindy led Gratis to the rail. She eyed him, wondering if someone so young could be experienced enough to handle the high-spirited racehorse. But, she reminded herself, she had been a young jockey once, too, and she had proven herself capable of riding just about any type of horse on the track.

She smiled at the jockey. "Welcome to Tall Oaks," she said.

7

"You folks have a pretty impressive facility," the young man said. He extended his right hand to Cindy. "I'm Miles Moyer."

"Hi, Miles," she greeted him. "I'm—"

But the rider shook his head. "I know who you are," he interrupted. "I used to watch you race in New York when I was a kid."

At thirty-two, Cindy hardly felt old, but Miles's words made her feel ancient. She tried not to let his comment bother her. "This is Gratis," she said, nodding toward the handsome bay colt, who stood quietly beside her.

"He's really a good-looking horse," Miles commented. "Are you ready for me to take him onto the track?" He held his hand out so that Gratis could sniff at his fingertips. The colt tossed his head impatiently and tugged at the lead, dancing his hindquarters around as he tried to edge closer to the track.

Ben stood near the rail, watching closely as Cindy gave Miles a boost onto Gratis's back. She kept a tight grip on the lead line, releasing the colt only after she had led him through the gap and onto the track. Then she joined Ben at the rail and held her breath, keeping her fingers crossed as Miles started Gratis at a steady walk along the outside edge of the track.

"He's still on," she murmured as the horse and rider reached the curve in the oval.

"Shh," Ben whispered. "You'll jinx them."

No sooner had he spoken than Gratis suddenly flung his head up and reared, striking at the air with his hooves. Miles leaned forward and hung on until Gratis dropped his front legs, landing with a jarring thud. The colt followed up with a buck that pitched the jockey onto his neck.

"Oh, no," Cindy groaned as the colt suddenly wheeled and bolted, dumping the rider onto the firm footing that Ben had recently had installed on the track.

She took a step toward the fallen rider, then hesitated, looking after the runaway colt.

"I'll see to your jockey," Ben said. "You handle Gratis." He strode toward Miles, who was staggering to his feet, and Cindy ducked under the rail to cut across the infield. As she started after Gratis, a slight figure darted onto the far side of the track and stepped into the path of the galloping horse.

Cindy broke into a run, afraid the colt would run

right over Wolf, the exercise rider she had hired shortly after coming to work at Tall Oaks. But Wolf flung his arms into the air, and to Cindy's surprise, Gratis skidded to a stop just a few feet from a sure collision. Wolf caught Gratis's reins, and she exhaled a deep sigh of relief.

She heard Ben call to her, and she turned in time to see Miles limping away. She walked back across the infield, meeting Ben at the inside rail.

"Another one bites the dust," Ben said, shaking his head. "We've got a serious problem, Cindy. If you can't get a jockey who can stay on that horse, how are we going to race him in the Kentucky Derby?"

Cindy sighed. "I know, Ben," she said. "The only rider who's ever done well with him was Christina, and I can't exactly ask her to race him."

Christina Reese, the daughter of another well-known jockey, Ashleigh Griffen, and her husband, Mike Reese, lived at Whitebrook, where her parents raised some of the top Thoroughbreds in the country. A skilled jockey, Christina had her own colt running in the Kentucky Derby. Wonder's Star, who shared the same dam as Champion, was a strong contender for the race.

"I agree," Ben said, then pointed at Wolf, who was

10

leading Gratis along the track. "Wolf doesn't seem to have any problem handling Gratis. What about him?"

"Wolf?" Cindy raised her eyebrows in surprise, then shook her head. "He isn't even an apprentice jockey. We can't put him on a horse in the Kentucky Derby."

Ben shrugged. "Then we'd better hope for a miracle." He sighed.

The sound of an engine caught Cindy's attention. She turned to see Ashleigh Griffen's car pulling up the drive. Cindy felt her mood lighten a little. Ashleigh had been Cindy's friend and mentor from the time Cindy, a runaway orphan, had been discovered hiding in one of the barns at Whitebrook Farm.

But the driver who climbed from the car was taller than Ashleigh, with red-brown hair and a bright smile. *What a coincidence*, Cindy thought. *I was just thinking about Ashleigh's daughter, and now here she is.* She waved to Christina as the passenger door opened and a petite blonde exited the car.

"Yo! Tall Oaks people," Melanie Graham called, hurrying toward the track. "We've come to check out the competition!"

Melanie, Christina's cousin, was also a skilled jockey with a filly running in the Derby. Perfect Image had been bred at Tall Oaks and was incredibly fast. Cindy wasn't surprised the filly was going to compete against the colts that normally held the field at Churchill Downs on Derby day.

"Hi, girls," Cindy said when the pair reached the track. She tilted her head toward Wolf and Gratis. "I'm afraid there isn't much to see as far as the competition goes."

"Gratis chased off another jockey, right?" Christina said, gazing at the big bay.

Cindy nodded, scrubbing at her forehead with her fingertips. "I don't know what we're going to do."

Wolf stopped Gratis at the rail, and the colt shoved his nose at Christina, snuffling at her loose hair.

"Hey, bad boy," she crooned, blowing softly into his nose. "What's your problem?"

"He needs a jockey who's smarter than he is," Wolf said, glancing at Cindy. "The last guy didn't know the first thing about riding a horse like Gratis." He gave the colt's neck a pat. Gratis bobbed his head vigorously, and Wolf grinned. "See?" he said. "He agrees with me."

Cindy ignored the exercise rider. Wolf didn't hesitate to share his low opinions of the jockeys and grooms Gratis had chased off. Cindy wished he would just do the job he'd been hired to do and keep his mouth shut. "He needs someone like you, Chris," she said.

"It took me some time to get him figured out," Christina replied. Cindy had seen Christina ride Gratis in New York during Belmont's winter racing season. That was before Ben had bought the colt, along with all the other stock at Tall Oaks. Christina had done well with Gratis, but Cindy knew that had come only after several disastrous attempts to control his behavior.

"I don't have any trouble with him," Wolf said, reaching up to smooth the young stallion's forelock. "I ride him every day."

"It takes years to become a successful jockey," Cindy said, trying to keep her voice neutral. Wolf seemed to have an unrealistic image of his skills and abilities. "Being able to ride is only the beginning," she reminded him.

Wolf looked at her evenly. "I could do it," he said.

"Not in time to ride in the Derby," Cindy retorted. "There are jockeys who spend years learning the trade and never get good enough to ride in the big races." She should know. She'd worked herself sick to become one of the top jockeys on the East Coast, but she'd never had a chance to race in any of the Triple Crown series. An old shoulder injury had ended her career just when she was reaching the top.

"I'm good enough," Wolf said.

The young rider's cockiness irritated Cindy, but she let the argument drop. Maybe after Wolf had proven himself over the next year or so as an exercise rider she'd consider helping him test for his apprentice license, but not after only a few weeks of riding for the farm.

When Gratis pawed nervously at the ground, Cindy looked from the colt to Christina. "He's all ready for a ride," she said. "Why don't you take him around the track a few times?"

"I'd love to," Christina said. "My helmet is in the car. I'll be right back."

"Are you and Image ready for the Derby?" Cindy asked Melanie.

Melanie nodded. "It's kind of overwhelming to be riding the only filly in the race," she said. "Image is really going to get a chance to show her stuff on the track in May." Melanie rubbed a fading bruise on her forehead. "Lucky for me the doctor cleared me to race again."

Melanie had been banged up pretty badly in a recent car accident in the Blazer she shared with Christina. She had started riding again only a few days earlier.

Cindy smiled. "I'm glad you're all right," she said. "It's going to be exciting to see you and Image on the track." She wished Melanie and Christina only the best with their Thoroughbreds, but more than anything she wanted to see Gratis come out the winner. She cast Ben a quick glance. It would be so exciting to see the handsome farm owner's expression when his own colt won the Kentucky Derby.

Christina returned, her helmet in place. Ben gave her a leg up into the saddle. "Have a safe ride," he said without a hint of a smile.

Christina grinned down at him. "Riding Gratis is *never* safe," she replied as Wolf released the lead line. Christina turned the colt and started along the rail. Gratis gave a few experimental bucks, but Christina quickly got him moving forward.

Cindy gave a little sigh and wiggled her shoulder. "I

wish *I* could take him around a time or two," she said softly. "I bet he'd be a lot of fun to ride."

Ben frowned at her. "You know better than that, Cindy," he said firmly. "The doctor's orders were very clear: Stay off the track. You don't want to do any more damage to that shoulder of yours."

Cindy frowned. "No," she agreed, "I don't. But it hasn't bothered me for months. I'm sure I could handle Gratis."

Cindy's shoulder had been injured so badly by her years of racing, it had taken an operation to repair her torn rotator cuff. The surgeon had made it very clear that any stress might cause her to lose the range of motion that surgery had restored.

"Look at Chris," Melanie said, pointing at the track.

Cindy forgot her shoulder and looked at Christina, who had moved Gratis into a gallop along the backstretch. Christina crouched over the colt's powerful shoulders, the reins taut in her hands as Gratis stretched out and ran. His long strides quickly brought him through the turn, and as they raced by, Christina gave the group at the sidelines a broad smile.

"He's awesome!" she yelled as they galloped away.

Melanie looked at her watch and gasped in dismay. "Chris and I need to get going," she told Cindy and Ben. "Ashleigh only let us use her car because we promised to run some errands for her."

"How long will it be before the Blazer is out of the shop?" Cindy asked.

Melanie turned pink. "It was in bad shape," she said. "But I hope it'll be ready by next week." She looked back at the track as Christina galloped Gratis into the turn again.

"Hey, Chris!" she called, holding her arm up and pointing at her watch. "We have to go!"

Christina slowed Gratis, who pranced to a stop, snorting and blowing. "He's all worked up now," she said to Cindy. "I should cool him down for you."

"Wolf can walk him out," Cindy said.

"That was some good riding," Wolf said to Christina, catching Gratis's headstall as she hopped from the colt's back. "How long have you been racing?"

"I got my license a year ago," Christina said.

"And you're racing in the Derby?" Wolf asked, giving Cindy a tight-lipped smile. "I guess it doesn't take everyone years to get good enough to ride in the Triple Crown races."

Cindy gritted her teeth. "Christina had a lot of experience before she ever tested for her license," she said.

"That's true," Christina said to Wolf as she gave Gratis a pet. "I had some good teachers." She turned to Cindy. "Good luck finding a jockey," she said.

"Thanks for coming by," Ben said, smiling.

"We'll see you later," Christina replied, unbuckling her helmet as she and Melanie headed for the car.

Ben turned to Wolf. "Do you need a leg up?"

"No, sir," Wolf said quickly. Before Cindy could tell him just to walk Gratis out on the lead, Wolf vaulted onto the colt's back and started him along the rail at an easy jog.

After just a few strides, Gratis tried to yank the reins from Wolf's grip and wheel around. Before Gratis could get away from him, Wolf gave the colt's sides a sharp rap with his heels and tightened his grip on the reins, driving Gratis forward.

Cindy shook her head as she watched Wolf fight the colt for a few minutes. "I don't know what I'm going to do with that horse," she said to Ben, who stood beside her at the rail. After a few more attempts to take control away from his rider, Gratis settled down. Cindy gnawed at her lower lip as she watched them walk briskly along the track.

"You look awfully deep in thought," Ben said.

"I'm racking my brain to think of a top-notch jockey we can get to ride Gratis for us." Cindy replied.

"Let me know what you come up with," Ben replied. "I need to get up to the house. I'm waiting for a call from Dubai. Taking over my father's business has been more work than I ever expected it to be." Because of health problems, Ben's father had recently retired, leaving Ben to manage the family's enterprises from his new home in the United States.

"How are your parents?" Cindy asked.

"My mother is fine, and she says Father seems to be doing much better now that he's retired," Ben said. "The last time we spoke he sounded good." He paused, gazing across the track at Wolf and Gratis. "I still think you should consider letting Wolf jockey Gratis."

"Let's not have that discussion again, please," Cindy said. Ben was charming and handsome, and he could run an international business without batting an eye. But he didn't know what it took to make a good jockey. That was her job.

"Fine," Ben said, and left the track. As he walked away, Cindy groaned to herself. The problem was, where was she going to find a qualified jockey in time for the race? And—even more important—a qualified jockey who could handle Gratis?

2

Cindy stayed at the rail for several minutes after watching Wolf cool Gratis out. The late April sun felt good, and she enjoyed the cheerful singing of the birds that flocked in the oak trees lining the drive. Gazing around the farm, she drank in the view of the rolling green fields, neatly fenced with gleaming white rails. She deeply inhaled the fresh air and let out a contented sigh.

It was so wonderful to be living on a horse farm again. She didn't miss her tiny apartment in Elmont, New York, one bit. After twelve years of crowds, concrete, and the fast-paced life she had lived for so long, the quiet and the wide open spaces of Kentucky felt like heaven.

There weren't many horses at Tall Oaks right now. Most of the farm's paddocks were empty, and Cindy dreamed of a day when there would be countless mares and foals filling the barns and pastures of her new home. The previous owner had run into financial troubles and sold off much of the stock before Ben bought the stable. Ben had spent the last several months restoring and repairing the facility. Cindy enjoyed helping him create the type of stable she had always dreamed of. Working with Ben and managing Tall Oaks almost made up for not being able to race anymore.

Cindy walked away from the track far enough to where she could see Champion grazing in his paddock. The sight of the handsome chestnut stallion made her smile. As much as she loved being in Kentucky, having Champion back was the best thing of all. She had missed the stallion more than she ever realized during all the years he was in Dubai.

Cindy was looking forward to the Keeneland sale in the fall. With Ben's backing, she would be able to select some of the top fillies being auctioned. Within a few years Tall Oaks would be producing stock with the best Thoroughbred blood in the country running through their veins. And if things went smoothly for Gratis in the Derby, she thought, turning her attention back to the track, the farm would have the prestige of owning a second Kentucky Derby winner, too.

She returned to the track to watch Wolf walking Gratis along the rail. The young exercise rider sat tall in the saddle, looking very smug as he rode the colt. Cindy sighed. Next fall and the world-famous Keeneland auction were a long way off. Right now she needed to solve her problem of finding a jockey for one well-bred, incredibly fast, but frustratingly bad-mannered bay colt. She mentally ran through the list of jockeys she knew, but any of the ones she would have liked to ride Gratis were already named on horses for the Derby.

"I'll find someone to ride him," she said firmly, as though saying the words out loud could make it true.

"I really could handle Gratis in the Derby," Wolf said suddenly, stopping the colt in front of her and dropping to the ground lightly. He rubbed the colt's glistening neck fondly.

"You've never shared the track with ten other horses," Cindy insisted.

"I could still do it," the exercise rider said, sounding very sure of himself. He swept an unruly lock of brown hair back from his forehead and stared at Cindy. "I know I could handle that race."

"Right," Cindy drawled. "And I could fly if I really wanted to." She ran a hand along Gratis's muscular shoulder. "He's cool enough to put up," she told Wolf. "Brush him out and be sure to rub his hooves down with treatment before you turn him out."

"I know how to take care of him," Wolf said. "And I know how to handle him. I should be his jockey." With that he turned away and led the colt toward the barns.

"There's a fine line between being overly confident and just plain arrogant," Cindy called after him, but Wolf didn't appear to hear her.

When he disappeared into the barn, Cindy stalked to the caretaker's cottage. When she had moved to Tall Oaks, Cindy had taken up residence in the cozy little house located close to the barns. Tiny compared to the mansion where Ben lived, the cottage still seemed spacious compared to the cramped apartment in New York.

Wolf's insistence that he was good enough to jockey

Gratis was going to make her crazy, Cindy thought as she sat down at her desk to look up some jockeys' phone numbers. Didn't Wolf realize how much work it took to get a shot at racing in the Kentucky Derby? She'd exhausted herself trying to reach that goal. She couldn't believe that Wolf thought he could simply hop on a horse and gallop to victory.

She flipped through her address book. Maybe someone from her days at Belmont could come down and race Gratis for Tall Oaks. The colt's increasingly bad reputation in Lexington wasn't going to help her find a good rider for him. So far Gratis had scared off four potential jockeys. And she had lost count of the number of grooms the colt had chased away. "Gratis," she muttered to herself, "you're almost more trouble than you're worth."

She found the number for Tommy Turner, a jockey who was a good friend of Ashleigh and Mike. He was in Florida for the racing season, but maybe he'd come up to ride for Tall Oaks. Tommy had a way with difficult horses, and with any luck, he'd be willing to race the colt.

But before she could pick up the phone, a loud

knocking on the front door distracted her. Cindy hurried through the living room and swung the door open, sure Wolf had followed her to the house to press his argument that he should race Gratis. She took a deep breath, prepared to send him back to the barn to clean stalls, but when she saw her visitor, Cindy's words died in her throat.

Ben stood in the doorway, his hand raised to knock again.

"Come on in," Cindy said, stepping back so that he could enter the cottage. She glanced behind her. It was a good thing she'd felt unusually domestic that morning and cleaned the house before going to the barns—usually there were at least a couple of pairs of discarded socks and a few dishes cluttering the floor and coffee table. She didn't want Ben to think she was a total slob.

"I wish you would stop encouraging Wolf," she told Ben as he followed her into the cottage. "Every time you tell him he's doing such a great job with Gratis, he gets more convinced that he should be the jockey of the year. He's already got an ego that weighs more than he does."

Ben shrugged. "He does have a way with that colt," he said. "You can't deny that, Cindy."

"But being able to handle a colt on an empty track doesn't mean he can manage a race, let alone the Kentucky Derby."

Ben nodded in understanding. "But if you don't find a jockey within the next few days, our plans for the race will have to be scrapped."

"It's getting to be a tough assignment," Cindy said, sinking onto the soft leather couch Ben had bought to furnish the cottage. "Gratis is gaining a huge reputation as a problem horse."

"Speaking of problems," Ben said, looking distressed, "we have something else to deal with." He settled onto the sofa beside her and leaned back.

"What is it?" Cindy asked, frowning at the grim expression on Ben's face.

"I just got a call from Brad Townsend," Ben said.

Cindy felt her stomach tense. The hairs on the back of her neck prickled as though a cold wind had blown over her. Anything to do with Brad Townsend had to be bad news. The egotistical, calculating owner of

Townsend Acres was always trying to make trouble, but usually his schemes involved Whitebrook. What could he possibly want with Tall Oaks?

Townsend Acres had owned Ashleigh's Wonder, the Derby-winning mare that Ashleigh Griffen had saved as a sickly foal. After Brad's father, Clay, had presented Ashleigh with half ownership in Wonder and all her offspring, Brad had been furious. He had never stopped trying to interfere in the care and training of Wonder and her jointly owned foals. With his scheming and manipulations, Brad had caused more than his share of problems.

She had been relieved when Brad sold Christina his interest in Wonder's Star, the last foal out of Ashleigh's Wonder, the previous winter. The sale had severed any ties between Townsend Acres and Whitebrook. Now Cindy was troubled by the thought that Brad had somehow found a way to hold something over Ben.

"Tell me he's going to sell you Celtic Mist," Cindy said. The Townsend Acres colt was a strong contender for the Kentucky Derby. Brad and his wife, Lavinia, had enjoyed many moments in the winner's circle thanks to the talented gray's performances on the track.

Ben smiled distractedly. "Brad sell me his prize colt? I think not," he said. "His call involves one of our horses."

Cindy shook her head in confusion. "Brad doesn't have any control over Tall Oaks." She raised her eyebrows and gave Ben a half smile. "You didn't lose the farm in some poker game, did you?"

Ben gave a little laugh and shook his head. "I'd never play poker with a snake like Brad," he said, then fell silent for a minute.

"Then what is it?" Cindy demanded, tension creeping up her back and spreading into her neck. Her shoulder started to throb a little, and she scowled. Leave it to Brad to make her shoulder ache, even though he was nowhere near her.

Ben exhaled slowly and sat up straight, looking into Cindy's eyes. "The problem has to do with Champion."

Cindy went rigid. She narrowed her eyes, feeling her heart sink. "What could Brad possibly have on Champion?" she demanded. "Clay Townsend sold his interest in Champion to your father years ago."

Ben rose and walked across the room, stopping near a wall Cindy had covered with photos of racehorses. A little table against the wall displayed figurines of famous Thoroughbreds. Ben picked up a glass statue of Secretariat and turned it over and over, avoiding Cindy's eyes. She felt herself becoming more tense as Ben's silence stretched on for several seconds. Finally he replaced the figurine and looked up at her, his dark eyes troubled.

"Brad says he has papers that show the sale of Champion to the al-Rihanis was never completed," he said. "According to Brad, Townsend Acres still owns the stallion, and they want him back."

3

"No!" Cindy breathed the word in a horrified gasp. The thought of losing Champion after just being reunited with him froze her for a moment. Her heart thudded dully in her chest. She had missed the stallion when he was in Dubai, but at least she knew he'd been well loved by Sheik al-Rihani and treated like royalty there. Who knew what Brad would do with Champion if he got him to Townsend Acres? He considered his Thoroughbreds to be commodities, not living creatures with brains and feelings. How could this have happened? She stared across the room at Ben for what seemed like an eternity.

As Ben took a step toward her, the numbness left

her in a flash, and Cindy leaped from the sofa and dashed for the door.

"Cindy, wait!"

But before Ben had finished speaking, Cindy was outside and racing toward the paddocks. She slowed when she saw Champion still standing in the middle of the pasture, his head turned toward her with a curious expression. She felt a little foolish, but in her panic, she had imagined Brad might already have taken the horse away. Seeing Champion safe in the field calmed her a little, and she stopped, trying to slow her racing heart. She heard footsteps behind her and turned to see Ben hurrying down the path, an anxious look on his face.

"Why did you run out?" he asked when he reached her.

"I just . . . I thought maybe . . ." But the words sounded so lame that she shook her head. "I panicked," she finally admitted, then started walking toward the paddock, Ben at her side. Champion stretched his graceful neck, yawned, shook himself from head to tail, then ambled toward the fence.

Ben leaned against the fence rail while they waited for Champion to cross the paddock. "For a minute there it felt like Dubai all over," he said in a soft voice.

"What do you mean?" Cindy asked, her gaze focused on Champion.

"When you left my father's stables so abruptly," Ben said. "I understand why you needed to return to the States, but when you stormed out without an explanation, never to return, I was so upset . . . I thought I'd never get over it."

Slowly Cindy lifted her chin and stared up at Ben. "I'm sorry," she murmured. "I heard you telling your father that women didn't belong on the track and—"

Ben raised his hand, and she fell silent. "I know what you heard," he said, shaking his head. "We've been over that. I was being sarcastic. I never thought you shouldn't be a jockey. I knew from the first time I saw you ride at Belmont that you belonged on a racehorse. I didn't understand why my father couldn't see it as clearly as I could."

A weak smile pulled at Cindy's mouth. "Thanks, Ben," she said. Champion reached the fence and pushed his nose at Cindy. She rubbed her hand along his smooth muzzle, tickling the silky-soft corner of his nose with her fingertips. The stallion flared his nostrils, inhaling her scent deeply, then lipped at her fingers.

"Sorry, boy," she said, patting his neck. "I was in such a hurry to see you that I forgot to bring a treat." She sighed and turned her attention back to Ben. "I'm ready to listen now," she said, forcing a calmness she didn't feel into her voice.

Ben worked his jaw for a moment, then frowned. "Brad will be coming by tomorrow," he said. "As I said, he claims to have found some papers that prove Champion was never legally taken out of the United States."

"But that can't be," Cindy protested, running a protective hand along Champion's sleek shoulder. "Clay Townsend was all for the sale. He needed the money more than he wanted Champion at that time."

Ben nodded. "We'll just have to see what nasty little tricks Brad has up his sleeve," he said. He gazed down at Cindy and offered her a slight smile. "We won't give up Champion without a fight. I promise you that, Cindy."

"What about your father?" Cindy asked, hope springing to life inside her. "He has the bill of sale, doesn't he?"

Ben looked solemn. "I called home as soon as I

heard from Brad," he said. "On top of everything else, my mother informed me that Father was admitted to the hospital this morning. Mother says he is only there under observation, but the doctor doesn't want him disturbed. As soon as he can, she'll have him call. In the meantime, we have no proof that Champion is solely ours. And if the papers Brad has are valid, there is nothing my father can do about it."

"I'm sorry about your father," Cindy said, suddenly feeling selfish as she realized the worried look on Ben's face wasn't just about Champion. "Do you need to go back to Dubai to be with your family?"

"No," Ben replied. "There's nothing I can do there. If my mother needs me, she'll let me know."

"If there's anything I can do . . ." Cindy's voice trailed off. During the year she had spent in the UAE, she had had several run-ins with Ben's father over her riding the racehorses he owned, but she had thought the world of Ben's mother, Zahra.

Ben nodded. "If I need to go home, I know Tall Oaks will be left in good hands," he said.

"Thanks for the vote of confidence," she said, giving him a smile. "Don't worry about anything here."

"I won't—you can handle it all if you need to," Ben said, smiling back. "And I'll do everything I can to make sure Champion is safe here."

"Thank you, Ben. I don't know what I'd do if I lost him again," she said softly, her hand still resting on Champion's shoulder.

Ben looked at the stallion, then at Cindy again, his gaze lingering on her face. "I know how you feel," he said.

Cindy didn't say anything, but she felt another blush start to warm her face.

"Hey!" At the sound of Wolf's voice, she looked toward the barn. The exercise rider was crossing the grounds in their direction.

"I suppose he's going to tell me what Gratis's feed rations should be now," she muttered. "The way he spouts off, you'd think he was a veteran jockey and trainer."

"He really does care about the colt," Ben said gently, giving Cindy an amused look.

"It seems to me he cares more about his own bloated ego," Cindy replied, then turned to face Wolf.

"Some guy called the barn," Wolf said when he reached Cindy and Ben. "He said that he's a jockey's agent and you should call him back to schedule a tryout for Gratis."

"Where's the phone number?" Cindy asked.

Wolf shrugged. "I left the message on your desk in the barn office," he said, pouting a little. "I didn't know you wanted me to hand-deliver it."

Cindy pinched her lips together and nodded. "Thank you," she said. "I'll deal with it."

"Whatever," Wolf said, and turned away, his shoulders rigid as he walked back to the barn.

"He really isn't a bad kid," Ben said.

"I didn't say he was," Cindy said. "He just acts like a know-it-all far too often for me."

Ben raised his shoulders in a shrug. "I trust your knowledge and judgment as far as your employees go."

Cindy smiled. "Don't worry, Ben. I'm not going to fire Wolf. At least not until I can find another exercise rider for Gratis."

"That's your call," Ben said. "I'll leave you to manage the stables. Right now I need to return to the house and take care of a few other things."

"And I'll go call that agent," Cindy said.

Ben headed for the house as Cindy gave Champion

37

one last pet, then strode toward the barn. Maybe Ben saw some qualities in Wolf that she didn't, but Ben didn't deal with him every day, either. She didn't appreciate Wolf's smart mouth whenever she gave him instructions. He was too sure of himself. Cindy knew that could be a disaster waiting to happen. She'd seen terrible wrecks on the track caused by riders who didn't know as much as they gave themselves credit for. There had to be another exercise rider in Lexington who could handle Gratis and who would be easier to get along with.

She found the agent's message in the middle of her desk, written in Wolf's untidy scrawl on the bottom of an invoice that she needed to pay. Annoyance flared in her, but she squelched it and sat down to pick up the phone. Ben liked Wolf, and the rider did get along with Gratis. He had that much going for him, anyway.

In a few minutes she had an appointment set for the agent to come to the farm with one of the jockeys he represented. "Tomorrow morning would be fine," she said hopefully. Maybe this jockey would be able to manage Gratis.

After finishing the phone call, she walked out to the colt's turnout. When Gratis saw her he flung his head in the air and whinnied, then trotted to the fence. Cindy reached out to pat him, but the colt tried to nip her fingers. "Stop that!" she snapped, narrowing her eyes and trying to look fierce.

Gratis pulled his head back and looked at her, wide-eyed.

"You're a bully!" she scolded him. "If you don't settle down and act like a gentleman Thoroughbred instead of some renegade mustang, I might just have Ben sell you to a rodeo show. How would you like that?"

Gratis snorted and bobbed his head vigorously, as though to say he didn't care. Cindy shook her head in disgust. "If you scare off another jockey," she told the colt, "that is exactly what I'm going to do."

Gratis bumped her arm with his nose, then, with another loud snort, wheeled away and galloped across the field. Cindy forgot her annoyance as she watched him run, awed by the colt's power and grace. Not getting a jockey to race him in the Derby would be a terrible waste of talent. As she watched him gallop around the paddock, she could see the cues he gave before he spun to the side, the way his ears flicked before he gave a little buck.

She could handle him, she realized. Gratis didn't intimidate her, and she could see how predictable he was. She wiggled her shoulder thoughtfully. It didn't bother her much anymore, and with some exercise she could regain her strength quickly. She imagined herself on the powerful bay, coming out of the gate at Churchill Downs for the Kentucky Derby. But she quickly shook off the thought. Racing Gratis in the Kentucky Derby was a dream that would never come true for her.

She turned away from the paddock and headed for the office. As the stable manager and head trainer of Tall Oaks, she had a lot of other work to do. Fantasizing about racing in the Kentucky Derby was a waste of her time.

The following morning she was at the barn before daylight. "Be sure you put extra vitamins in Champion's feed rations," she told Elizabeth, the stable hand who had been working at Tall Oaks before Ben bought the stable. "I want him in the best condition possible when breeding season comes around."

Elizabeth nodded knowingly. "Having a Triple

Crown-winning stallion is certainly going to help rebuild the stable's reputation as a top-notch farm," she said, smiling. Besides Champion, Khan, a handsome bay, was the only stallion at Tall Oaks. If they could find the right jockey for Gratis, he could be the farm's second Triple Crown winner, and Tall Oaks would gain a lot of prestige and attention in the racing world.

"I'll have Beckie take care of the stallions today," Elizabeth said, nodding toward a slender blond girl who was wheeling a cart of soiled bedding down the aisle. "She's really working out well, Cindy. I'm glad you hired her."

Beckie, the first employee Cindy had hired at Tall Oaks, smiled cheerfully as she passed Cindy and Elizabeth. "Good morning," she greeted Cindy in a pleasant voice colored with an Australian accent.

"As soon as you're done with that," Elizabeth said, nodding toward the full cart, "I have some other things for you to do."

"I'm almost done with the stalls," Beckie replied. "I'll be right back."

Cindy had to agree with Elizabeth. Beckie was a great employee, hardworking and always pleasant and agreeable. Cindy wished some of the girl's personality would rub off onto Wolf. Ben was right. The kid was good with the horses, but his attitude frustrated her no end.

As Elizabeth walked away to continue her own morning's work, Cindy headed for the practice track. When she reached the oval, Wolf had already saddled Gratis and was preparing to take the colt out for his morning work.

"Just give him an easy warm-up," Cindy told the rider. "The jockey should be here in about half an hour."

Wolf rolled his eyes at her, then vaulted onto Gratis's back. "I know how to warm him up," he muttered, looking down at her.

Cindy hissed through her teeth, fighting down the urge to order Wolf off the colt. She could take Gratis on the track herself. But the exercise rider turned the colt and rode onto the track.

Cindy watched from the rail, trying to find fault with Wolf's handling of the feisty horse. But for every stunt Gratis tried to pull, Wolf was a step ahead of him.

He walked and then jogged the colt around the track for several minutes.

Cindy focused on Gratis's moves and made a list in her head of the workouts she wanted for him over the next several days. She wanted so badly for Gratis to do well in the Derby, to reestablish Tall Oaks as one of the top stables in Kentucky. That was the least she could do for Ben.

When the jockey and his agent arrived, Cindy's hope that this rider would be the right one for Gratis faded instantly.

"I'm Rob Randall," the agent said, giving Cindy a brief nod. The toothpick the agent was rolling in one corner of his mouth distracted Cindy. She almost laughed at the way he worked his jaw busily, keeping the splinter of wood in motion. "This is Larry Mc-Reavy," he added, slowing his jaw long enough to introduce Cindy to the man standing beside him.

"Hi," Cindy said, extending her hand to Larry. The jockey pumped it energetically, then turned his attention to the track, where Wolf was bringing Gratis along the far side of the track at a brisk trot.

"Is that the horse?" Larry asked. "He sure moves out nice."

Cindy frowned at him as she tried to recall whether she had ever heard his name before. "How many championship races have you ridden?" she asked Larry.

The jockey glanced at his agent, who puffed his chest out. "Larry has been riding on the West Coast," he said. "And very successfully, too. He hasn't had a chance to compete in any of the East Coast races."

"Oh." Cindy sighed. In other words, she told herself, Larry McReavy was a little-known jockey who was willing to take a chance with a problem horse to make his name on the East Coast racing circuit. And what better race than the renowned Kentucky Derby? She was tempted to send Rob and Larry away without the tryout, but she needed a jockey too badly. Instead she waved to Wolf, who brought Gratis to the rail.

"Let's see how you do with him," she said to Larry as Wolf dismounted.

The exercise rider held Gratis and gave the jockey an appraising look. "Are you sure you can handle him?" he asked.

"I've ridden lots of different horses," Larry said as

Rob stepped forward to give him a leg up onto Gratis's back.

Strike one, Cindy thought. Larry hadn't even introduced himself to the colt, to let Gratis get a sense of the person who was going to be controlling him on the track.

"Got him," Larry said, collecting the reins. He guided Gratis along the rail, keeping the colt at a walk.

Gratis seemed as meek as a lamb for the jockey, but Cindy didn't believe his act for a moment. She knew he would try something with the new rider. He always did.

"He's going to blow," Wolf muttered to Cindy. "He's going to spin left and buck." Even as the last word was leaving his mouth, Gratis made his move, doing exactly as Wolf had predicted.

Caught completely by surprise, Larry flew over Gratis's shoulder and rolled on the track. Gratis cantered away, and Wolf ducked under the rail to go after the horse.

Larry was shaking his head as he scrambled to his feet. "I've never had that happen before," he claimed. "He didn't even give any warning."

"Try him again," the agent urged, but Cindy shook her head.

"Never mind," she said. "I don't think we'll be needing your services, Mr. McReavy."

"That's fine by me," the jockey exclaimed, walking rapidly past Cindy toward the agent's car. "That horse is unmanageable. You'll never find someone to ride him in a race."

As she watched the car go down the driveway, Cindy sighed. She was afraid that Larry, inexperienced as he was, was right. And as close as they were to the Derby, the chances of finding the right jockey grew slimmer by the day.

4

Wolf stopped Gratis at the rail and dropped his chin, looking at Cindy from beneath his eyebrows. He shook his head in disgust. "If you keep bringing in worthless jockeys to ride him, he's never going to see the inside of the starting gate on Derby day."

"That's none of your business, Wolf," Cindy said. "I'll deal with finding a jockey. You just do your job, okay?"

"I could handle him in a race," Wolf said again.

"Drop it," Cindy snapped. The sound of a car coming up the drive drew her attention away from Wolf and Gratis. She turned to see a dark sports car cruise up to the house and stop. Brad Townsend, her least favorite person in the entire world, climbed from the car and paused to look around Tall Oaks before he strode to the house. In a moment the door opened and he disappeared inside.

Cindy thought about going up to the house to give Brad an earful of her feelings about him, but she knew it wouldn't help the situation. Besides, she was sure Ben wouldn't appreciate her getting in the middle of things. All she could do was hope Ben could bring Brad's plan of claiming ownership of Champion down with a resounding crash.

She heard movement behind her. When she turned back to the track, Wolf was on Gratis, jogging the horse along the rail again. She thought about calling him back. He didn't need to work the colt any longer, but as she watched, Gratis tried to buck.

Wolf quickly busied the colt, forcing him to weave back and forth the width of the track. Before long, Gratis was paying full attention to his rider again, and soon Wolf had him cantering smoothly up the backstretch. Cindy sighed in appreciation. Until she could find an exercise rider who could manage the horse, she knew she was stuck with Wolf.

She heard a door slam and glanced behind her to see Ben and Brad come out of the house. The two men paused on the wide porch. Brad stabbed his finger in the direction of Champion's pasture, then turned back to Ben, who had his arms folded across his chest. Cindy cringed, wishing fervently that Brad would just go away quietly, but she knew that wasn't going to happen.

When she heard another car coming up the driveway, Cindy groaned to herself. *What now?* she thought, but when she saw Ashleigh Griffen's sedan slowing near the barns, she almost smiled. She doubted Brad would be nearly as intimidating with Ashleigh there. As Champion's half owner, Ashleigh had been involved in the deal that sent Champion to the al-Rihanis' stable. Maybe she could set Brad straight on the facts.

Ashleigh and Christina climbed from the car and headed for the track. Christina pointed at Ben and Brad, and Ashleigh's jaw dropped when she saw Brad. She stared in that direction for a moment, then hurried toward Cindy.

Cindy smiled wanly at Ashleigh. "I am *so* glad to see you," she said.

Ashleigh glanced back at the two men, who were almost to the track, then frowned at Cindy. "What's Brad doing here?" she asked.

Cindy heaved a sigh. "You won't believe it when you hear it," she said. But before she could tell Ashleigh more, Ben and Brad had moved within earshot. Cindy could tell by the slump of Ben's shoulders that he didn't have good news. She took a deep breath, bracing herself for a confrontation with Brad.

"Gratis sure looks good," Christina commented. Cindy looked over to see Christina watching Wolf canter the colt around the oval.

"He sure does," Ashleigh said, her eyes riveted on the powerful bay. Gratis tossed his head, fighting Wolf to give him some slack in the reins. Wolf loosened his hold a fraction, and Gratis sped up. The colt was on the verge of breaking into a gallop.

"Wow," Ashleigh murmured. "He looks even better than he did last winter at Belmont, Cindy. I'd love to see him run again."

Cindy smiled at the admiring tone she heard in her friend's voice, and she was eager to show off Gratis's speed.

As Wolf and Gratis neared them, she waved, signaling Wolf to move the colt into a gallop. She saw the rider's face break into a huge grin. Wolf leaned forward, pushing his fisted hands up Gratis's neck. Gratis eagerly sped up, flying along the rail with ground-eating strides.

"Awesome," Christina murmured. She turned to Cindy, wide-eyed. "I knew he was fast when I rode him, but he looks even better now."

Cindy glanced over to see Ben standing at the rail, his eyes fixed on the running colt. On the other side of Ben, Brad Townsend was also staring at Wolf and Gratis, an intense frown darkening his face.

Cindy forgot about Gratis for a moment, thoughts of Brad's threat to take Champion crowding everything else from her mind. Wolf brought Gratis to a stop when they neared the gap in the rail. The bay colt was snorting and prancing as the rider dismounted.

"That was some impressive riding," Ashleigh told Wolf.

"It really was," Christina chimed in, nodding in approval.

"Thanks," Wolf said, his grin widening. "I'll go cool

him out now," he said, then led the sweating colt away from the track. Cindy turned her full attention to Ben and Brad.

Deep furrows creased Ben's brow, and his mouth was pressed into a tight line. Brad's expression was unreadable. He watched Wolf leading Gratis toward the barn, shaking his head slightly. Cindy eyed the manila envelope he held, then looked to Ben again.

Ben's attempt at an encouraging smile failed, and Cindy felt fear grip her chest, making it hard to breathe.

"The papers do appear to confirm what Brad said about Champion's sale," Ben said in a soft voice.

"What are you talking about?" Ashleigh snapped her head in Brad's direction, her eyes narrowing as she glared at him.

"Brad says his father never really sold Champion," Cindy explained.

"That's right," Brad said, holding up the envelope. "These documents prove it."

Cindy wanted to snatch the envelope from his hands and throw it in the manure pile behind the barn. Whatever was in that envelope had the power to take Champion away, and she wanted to destroy it.

"Clay would never renege on that kind of deal," Ashleigh said, keeping her steady gaze on Brad's face.

Brad's lips formed a cold sneer as he stared back at Ashleigh. "It doesn't matter what you think my father would or wouldn't do," he said, his voice hard and flat-sounding. "These documents confirm that the transfer papers were never properly completed." He shot Cindy a look, a cold smile curling the corners of his mouth. "Champion was taken away in such a hurry that no one ever bothered to finalize the sale."

"I don't believe that," Ashleigh said. "Your father sold his interest in Champion in good faith, Brad. What kind of stunt are you trying to pull here?"

"It isn't a stunt, Ashleigh." The way Brad said her name made Cindy's blood boil. Brad had always talked down to Ashleigh. He was always trying to remind her that she had been nothing until his father had gifted her with an interest in Wonder.

"Maybe Clay would say differently," Ashleigh said. "Have you called him, Ben?"

"He's traveling through Europe for the next six months," Brad cut in. "There's no way to reach him."

Six months? Cindy's heart sank. The only two people who could confirm Champion's ownership were Habib al-Rihani and Clay Townsend. With neither of them available to dispute Brad's claim, Champion's life at Tall Oaks was really in jeopardy.

"You don't happen to have a copy of the full sale record, do you?" Ben asked Ashleigh, sounding hopeful.

Ashleigh shook her head slowly. "I wasn't in any shape to deal with anything," she said with a sad sigh. "Clay handled all the paperwork."

Cindy ground her teeth together. At the time Champion had been sold, Ashleigh was in the hospital, recovering from losing her second child after Champion had run her over.

"The papers were never filed," Brad said, waving the hated envelope again. "Now we need to make arrangements to move the stallion to Townsend Acres, where he rightfully belongs."

"No," Cindy whispered, unable to believe this was really happening. She gripped the rail with both hands, afraid she would collapse if she let go.

Ben glared at Brad. "Not so fast," he said. "Champion isn't going anywhere until we can confirm your claim."

Brad didn't answer Ben. His attention was fixed on a point on the far side of the training track. Cindy looked up to see what had his interest, but all she saw was Wolf leading Gratis, now draped in a cooling sheet, around one of the smaller paddocks.

"Alydar and Affirmed," Brad muttered, his eyes locked on the sheeted bay colt.

Cindy's heart went cold. She knew Brad was referring to Gratis's bloodlines. Alydar and Affirmed had both raced in the Triple Crown series years earlier. With Affirmed on his sire's side and Alydar on his dam's, Gratis seemed to have inherited both stallions' racing talent.

She looked back at Brad. The envelope that contained proof of his ownership of Champion dangled from his hand, apparently forgotten as he watched Wolf walk Gratis back to the barn. Anger began to overcome her fear, and she fought back an overwhelming desire to rip the envelope from Brad's hands and order him to stay away from Tall Oaks, Champion, and Gratis. But that was up to Ben, not her.

She glanced at Ben, waiting for him to speak up, but his puzzled look made her realize that Brad's muttered words hadn't meant anything to him. She let go of the rail, keeping her fists clenched at her sides while she faced Brad.

"You don't have any claim to Gratis, Brad," she said sharply.

Brad slowly turned his attention to Cindy, his eyes cold and his expression calculating. "But I do have a claim on your precious Champion," he said, stretching his lips in a chilly smile. He looked at Ben, then jutted his chin toward the barn that Wolf had led Gratis into. "That bay is your Derby entry, right?"

"You know he is," Ben said evenly. "What does that have to do with your legal game over Champion's ownership?"

Brad raised his eyebrows. "I might have a proposition for you," he said.

Cindy wrapped her arms around herself, trying to ward off the chill that had settled over her.

Beside her, Ashleigh reached out and rested her hand lightly on Cindy's shoulder. She squeezed gently, trying to offer Cindy some small measure of comfort. Cindy was grateful for the gesture, but it didn't make her feel any less alone or less helpless in the face of Brad's ruthlessness.

"What's your proposal?" Ben said, his voice neutral.

"I'll give up my claim on Champion if you pull Gratis from the Derby," Brad said.

Cindy gaped at him. Pull Gratis from the Derby? "Forget it," she snapped before Ben could say anything. Gratis had a very good chance of winning the race, and the fame that win would bring to Tall Oaks would help the stable's status immensely. She knew Ben wanted to build the farm's reputation as a highly successful Thoroughbred facility, and it could be years before they had another colt of Gratis's caliber. Withdrawing Gratis from the Derby was out of the question.

Ben was shaking his head slowly. "Why would you want that?" he asked Brad, frowning in confusion.

Brad shrugged lightly. "I have my own reasons," he said. "I think it's a pretty generous offer. You'd better consider it." He smiled again, that hard, icy look sending a blast of coldness through Cindy. "It's the only way you're going to keep Champion here."

Cindy felt as though she were being torn in two.

When she had been in Dubai, Ben's father's dream had been to own an American-bred horse that could race in the Kentucky Derby, but he had never found the right horse. She knew how much it meant to Ben to be able to race Gratis for his father, as well as for the good it would do Tall Oaks. And now, with Habib al-Rihani's health problems, it seemed more important than ever to keep Gratis entered in the race. She couldn't let Brad take this away from Ben and his family.

"I'll be back tomorrow," Brad said. "I'll bring my attorney so we can discuss this situation. You really aren't in a position to bargain, al-Rihani. If you don't jump on my offer by then, I won't make it again." He turned and strode toward his sports car.

Cindy glared after him, her hands shaking as she struggled to contain her anger and frustration.

"What a *jerk*," Christina said from behind her.

"He does seem to bring his own unique brand of problems wherever he goes," Ben said. He sighed deeply, then gave Cindy a weak smile. "Unfortunately, there doesn't seem to be any way to dispute his claim on Champion." He pressed his lips together and looked across the paddocks at Champion. The stallion was basking in the morning sun.

Cindy followed his gaze. She couldn't believe the nightmare she was being plunged into. She couldn't stand giving up Champion for the second time in her life, but how could they not race Gratis?

"Brad has offered us a way to avoid giving up Champion," Ben said, his eyes still focused on the chestnut stallion.

Cindy darted a look at him. "We can't pull Gratis," she said.

"But Brad has put us in a difficult position," Ben countered, looking down at her.

"He sure has," Ashleigh said from behind Cindy. "He seems to have put you between the proverbial rock and a hard place."

"Unfortunately, yes." Ben exhaled and rubbed the back of his neck while he looked at the three women, then shook his head. "And right now I don't see a way out."

5

"That rat!" Christina exclaimed, watching Brad cruise slowly down Tall Oaks' drive. "How can he be so nasty?"

Ben looked steadily at Cindy. "We can pull Gratis from the Derby," he said. "We're not even sure he's going to be able to race."

"Forget it!" Cindy insisted. "Brad can't give us an ultimatum like that. He's playing a power game, and we can't let him get away with it!"

Ashleigh gave Cindy and Ben a quizzical look. "What do you mean, you're not sure about Gratis running?"

Cindy heaved a deep sigh. "We don't have a jockey for him," she admitted. "Yet, anyway."

Ashleigh raised her eyebrows in surprise. "But the race is so close."

"We know," Cindy said, sounding glum. She slumped against the track fence. "I'm still trying to find someone who can work with him, but it isn't looking very good."

"So we'll let Brad think he's won, Cindy," Ben said. "We'll keep Champion here, and maybe next year Tall Oaks will have a Derby contender that someone can actually handle in a race."

Cindy gazed at Christina. "You're sure you don't want to scratch Star from the race?" she asked, only half joking. "You're the one jockey Gratis really moves out for. With you on him, that colt would be a sure thing in the winner's circle."

Christina offered Cindy a weak smile. "I wish I could ride them both," she said, sounding sincerely regretful.

"I know," Cindy said, surprised by Christina's response. When she had been Christina's age, she wouldn't have given Gratis a second thought if she had owned a horse of Star's caliber. "You and Star have gone through a lot to get to this point. You both deserve your shot at the Derby."

61

Christina had nearly lost Wonder's Star to a virus the previous winter. Bringing him back to racing condition had been a long, hard struggle for Christina, but Star was in top form again and ready to race. Cindy knew how important the Derby was for both Christina and her horse. She could never seriously try to talk Christina out of racing Star.

"If it comes down to it," Cindy said, giving everyone a determined look, "I'll ride Gratis myself. We can't let Brad get away with this."

Ashleigh's eyes widened with alarm and her mouth fell open as she stared at Cindy. Ben's shocked look was almost a perfect match for Ashleigh's. If the situation hadn't been so serious, Cindy would have burst out laughing at both of them as they gaped at her.

"You're not riding!" they said at the same time.

Cindy rolled her eyes skyward and shook her head, then looked from Ashleigh to Ben. "My shoulder feels really good," she said. "I could handle one race."

"Not a chance," Ben said, folding his arms across his chest. "The doctors were very clear on that subject."

"You can't risk reinjuring yourself, Cindy," Ashleigh said. She rubbed her lower back thoughtfully. "I really messed my back up because I didn't stop racing when I should have. This is only one race," she went on, "but it might mean a lifetime of pain."

Ben nodded in agreement. "Ashleigh's right," he said.

Cindy grunted with frustration.

"What's wrong with Wolf?" Christina asked, looking at Cindy. "He handles Gratis a lot better than I ever did."

Cindy sighed as she looked at Christina. "Wolf doesn't even have his apprentice license," she said. "Besides, being able to exercise-ride doesn't mean he has a clue as to what it's like to race. And wouldn't it set the racing world on its ear if we put a totally inexperienced jockey in the Derby? I don't even know if the officials would allow it. We need someone with experience, and you all know it."

Ashleigh nodded slowly. "You have a point," she said. "But it can't be you, Cindy."

"We need to leave," Christina told her mother as she glanced at her watch. "We promised Sammy we'd stop by Whisperwood. I want to see the new jumper she bought. And I haven't visited Sterling in weeks."

Samantha Nelson, Cindy's sister, owned a show-jumping facility with her husband, Tor. Before Christina had started racing, she had had a promising future in three-day eventing with her gray mare, Sterling Dream. For years Christina had been dead set against racing; that had frustrated Ashleigh, whose life revolved around Thoroughbreds and the racetrack. Cindy had been surprised to learn that Christina had sold Sterling to the Nelsons when she began to pursue her racing career. But Christina's dedication to Star and developing her skills as a jockey had paid off. Cindy was impressed with how quickly Christina had taken to being a jockey and proven herself on the track by succeeding with difficult horses such as Gratis.

"If you know of any available jockeys who might be willing to give Gratis a try, give me a call," Cindy told Ashleigh as she and Christina prepared to leave.

Ashleigh looked doubtful, but she nodded. "I'll check around," she promised.

After Ashleigh and Christina left, Cindy turned to Ben and started to speak.

"No," he said before she even asked the question on her mind.

"How do you know what I was going to say?" she asked.

"I could see it in your face," Ben said. "You're not even going to take Gratis on the practice track." He gave her a dark look. "The colt may be well bred and he may be fast, but he isn't a safe horse for you to get on, Cindy."

Cindy gazed at the track, then to the distance where Champion was enjoying the sun. She loved being here, but life at Tall Oaks was tinged with a sadness she couldn't escape. "I miss riding so much," she said in a quiet voice.

"I'm sure you do," Ben said. "I understand how you feel, but it simply isn't something you can do anymore."

"Remember when we rode your father's saddle horses in Dubai?" Cindy asked, looking up at Ben. "The day we went to the market and you bought me the white scarf?"

"How could I forget that day?" Ben replied, smiling at the memory. "You wore that *gutrah* that same afternoon, when we rode to the beach. I thought you were the cutest blond-haired, blue-eyed Bedouin girl I had ever seen."

Cindy snorted. "I was the *only* blond-haired, blue-eyed Bedouin girl you'd ever seen."

"That too," Ben said, chuckling.

Cindy frowned thoughtfully. She and Ben had spent a memorable day at the *souq*, or market, wandering among the vendors' stalls and buying souvenirs, then later watching the camel races. Remembering the young camel jockeys made Cindy grin. The strange-looking mounts had been surprisingly graceful and swift, in spite of their ungainly appearance.

"I left all the Arabian tack I bought in Dubai behind when I came back to the States," she recalled. "I didn't figure I'd have a need for an embroidered velvet saddle at the racetrack, and calling a lead line a *megwad* and a headstall an *egal* certainly wouldn't have made me fit in at Belmont." She chuckled softly at the thought. Fitting in at Belmont had been enough of a challenge without doing things like that.

But remembering riding across the desert with Ben that day made her think of the beautiful *shoband* she had bought. The tasseled breast band had looked good on the Arabian gelding she had ridden. "I wonder whatever happened to all those things," she said, then

66

dismissed the thought with a wave of her hand. "It doesn't matter, anyway. It isn't like I'll ever ride again."

Ben raised his eyebrows. "What if you had a saddle horse?" he asked. "I thought the doctor was only keeping you off the racetrack."

Cindy expelled a snort of disgust. "That's right. But once you've competed on the racetrack, any other kind of riding seems a little too tame." She shook her head. "Why would I bother getting back in the saddle? Just to amble around some boring little paddock? I might as well go ride a merry-go-round horse."

Ben gave her a searching look. "I did bring your Arabian tack with me," he told her. "It's all in a box up at the house. I hesitated to return it to you because I was afraid it would remind you of your time in the UAE and how unhappy you were there."

Cindy gave Ben a look of surprise. "I was homesick and frustrated, but it wasn't twelve months of misery," she said. "I do have some good memories of the stable, and I made a few friends." She smiled to herself, remembering the young groom who had taken such good care of Champion. Kalim had forged a close bond with the horse almost immediately. Knowing that

Kalim was caring for Champion had made it less heart-rending for Cindy to leave Dubai.

"Kalim is quite grown-up now," Ben said. "He's attending college and studying veterinary medicine." He gazed at Cindy. "I also didn't want the tack to remind you that you can no longer ride the way you did then."

Cindy wiggled her shoulder. "My rotator cuff reminds me of that every day," she said, trying to keep the bitterness she felt out of her voice. "In fact, I have an appointment with the doctor tomorrow." She forced a smile for Ben. "Maybe he'll have a change of heart and agree that I'm fit to ride again."

"That would be great," Ben said, but his dark eyes didn't offer Cindy any encouragement. "If you do decide you want the things we bought at the *souq*, I'll have Elizabeth bring the box down from the house for you."

"Sure," Cindy said. "Even if I can't use them, they'd make interesting conversation pieces to decorate the cottage." She smiled. "And they'll always remind me of that day and how much fun it was to gallop across the desert and end up at the beach." She heard the wistful tone in her voice and felt her smile soften as she relived that long-ago ride. "Those Arabian saddle horses of your father's were such well-trained animals."

Ben nodded. "I've never been on one of the race-horses," he said. "But I know the saddle horses must seem quite tame compared to a Thoroughbred trained to race."

"That was one of the best times I remember of that whole year at your father's stable," Cindy said.

Ben smiled. "It was for me, too," he said, then glanced at his watch. "I need to return to the house," he told Cindy. "I have to put in a call to my father's attorneys in Dubai to see if they have any of the records that might prove Brad's claim is wrong." He gave Cindy an encouraging smile. "I will do everything I can to keep Champion where he belongs, here with you," he promised.

"Thank you, Ben," Cindy replied. As Ben strode away, Cindy turned back to look at the empty track. She missed riding so much; it felt like a deep ache all the way through her. The longing to be on a horse welled up inside her until she could hardly stand the feeling. But she didn't think a leisurely hack on a trail horse could ever make up for not being allowed to race.

She quickly turned from the track and headed for her office at the barn. There was no point standing around moping, she told herself firmly. At least she was able to work with the horses, even if she couldn't get back in the saddle.

6

"Your shoulder seems to have healed up nicely," the surgeon said, nodding in approval as he looked at the X rays hanging on the lighted screen in his office.

"So I could start racing again?" Cindy sat on the edge of her chair, looking from the pictures of her shoulder to the doctor. Maybe she could race Gratis after all.

But Dr. Klein dashed her hopes by shaking his head and frowning. "No," he said flatly, folding his arms across his chest. He gave Cindy a stern look. "The stress it would put on the repairs we've done would be too much."

Cindy sank back in her chair, weighted down by disappointment.

"But there is an upside," the doctor added, offering her an encouraging smile. "You have regained almost all your range of motion, and you seem to be functioning very well now. Be happy with what you can do, Cindy."

Cindy rose and gave him a quick, weak smile. Dr. Klein didn't know how much being on a racehorse meant to her. "I am," she said. "I appreciate what you've been able to do for me."

She left the office and walked to her car, trying to ignore her sense of loss. She had always clung to the hope that someday she might be able to get back on a racehorse, but it was never going to happen. She felt her heart tearing as she realized she was going to have to accept that reality.

She drove back to Tall Oaks, barely noticing the farms and the Thoroughbreds in the pastures that she passed on her way home. There seemed to be a dark cloud hanging over her that made it hard to see the beauty of the rolling fields and the elegance of the graceful horses grazing wherever she looked.

Finally Cindy released an exasperated sigh. "Snap out of it," she ordered herself out loud. She wasn't going to give in to self-pity now. She had a lot to be thankful for, starting with her family and friends. On top of that, she had a great job at a wonderful stable. She just had to keep thinking of the good things in her life.

When she pulled into the driveway and parked by the cottage, she glanced toward the barns and frowned. Someone had moved one of the horse trailers. It was hooked up to the farm's pickup and parked near the open door of one of the smaller barns, where mares brought in for breeding were normally kept. But breeding season was several months off, so why would the barn be open now?

She headed for her little house, eager to change from her slacks and blouse into jeans and a T-shirt. Then she would get down to the barn and find out what was going on.

As she started to open the cottage door, a horrible thought dawned on her and a sudden sick feeling gripped her. Cindy froze, her hand on the doorknob. Had Ben given in to Brad's demands to bring Champion back to Townsend Acres? Was that why the trailer was out, while they prepared to haul her beautiful stallion away? She started to wheel around, ready to rush to the barn and protect Champion.

But as she turned away from the house, a slim figure emerged from the barn. Beckie, the new groom, waved excitedly to Cindy as she jogged across the yard.

"Cindy, wait!" she called.

Cindy eyed the groom closely. Beckie didn't appear upset, which eased the tense knot in Cindy's stomach a little.

"What's going on?" Cindy asked when Beckie reached her. A grin was pulling at Beckie's mouth, and Cindy couldn't help but smile herself. The girl's enthusiasm and energy seemed to rub off on anyone she was around. Cindy's dark mood lightened. Hiring Beckie was one more good thing she could add to her list.

"There's something in the barn you have to see," Beckie said. She was struggling to sound serious, but Cindy could see a bright twinkle in the girl's eyes. She relaxed a little more. Beckie wouldn't be so upbeat if her news had to do with Champion leaving.

Her short bout of depression over her shoulder forgotten, Cindy followed Beckie across the yard. "Can you tell me what I'm going to see?" she asked.

Beckie shook her head vigorously. "It's a surprise," she said. "I promised Ben and Elizabeth I wouldn't tell. You can't even torture it out of me. You'll just have to wait and see."

Cindy laughed at Beckie's comments and started walking a little faster, eager to find out what was going on.

When they reached the doorway, Beckie swept her hand toward the interior of the barn, indicating that Cindy should walk inside. "Ta-da!" she exclaimed.

Cindy stopped just inside the barn, staring in disbelief at the horses standing crosstied in the wide aisle.

Elizabeth glanced up from where she was fastening the girth of a red velvet Arabian saddle onto a small gray mare. "Hi," she said, grinning at Cindy.

"That isn't a Thoroughbred," Cindy said, gaping at the delicate mare. "That's an Arabian."

"Very good," Ben said from where he stood beside a tall bay gelding, settling an English saddle on the horse's back. "It's good to know that the year in Dubai helped you learn how to identify one of our desert horses."

"What are they doing here?" Cindy demanded, walking slowly to the mare and holding her hand out. The mare stretched her nose, sniffing delicately at Cindy's outstretched fingers. Cindy stood quietly, letting the mare acquaint herself with the new human's scent. After a moment, the mare calmly licked Cindy's hand. Cindy smiled and gently rubbed the horse's soft gray nose. "You are really sweet," she said as the fine-boned gray raised her head to snuffle at Cindy's hair.

"So you like her?" Ben asked, giving the bay gelding a pat on the shoulder.

"She's so calm," Cindy said, stroking the mare's sleek neck.

"She's retired from a program for handicapped riders," Elizabeth said. "A friend of mine told me about her, and when Ben said he was looking for a gentle saddle horse, I knew Dove would be perfect for you."

Cindy gaped at Ben. "For me? But . . ." Her voice trailed off.

Ben nodded, his smile hesitant. "I know trail riding isn't the same thing as being a jockey, but I hoped you might be willing to give Dove a try anyway. But if you don't wish to, we can find her a new home."

Cindy wasn't sure if she wanted to laugh or cry. After the things she had said the day before, she'd thought Ben wouldn't push her about riding. But it dawned on her that she was glad he had. She felt a rush of gratitude toward Ben as she continued to stroke Dove's soft coat.

"It certainly won't be like racing," she said. "But since she's ready to go, I guess I'd better take her out." She smiled, looking into the Arabian's gentle eyes.

"Go change into some riding clothes," Elizabeth urged her. "Dove's waiting."

"I see that," Cindy said, stepping back to admire the way the Arabian tack looked on the mare. "She looks perfect." She grinned at Elizabeth and Beckie, then gave Ben a warm smile. "Thanks, everyone."

"Hurry up and get changed," Beckie urged her. "I can hardly wait to see you in the saddle."

Stunned by the excitement she felt at the idea of simply being on horseback, Cindy rushed back to the cottage. She quickly changed into jeans and paddock boots and soon was dashing out of the house. Ben had been so thoughtful, trying to make her happy. Her fond memory of their ride in the Arabian desert made it easier to think about trail riding, and sharing time on horseback with Ben gave her something special to look forward to.

When she reached the barn, the horses were outside. Ben was already in the saddle, the bay gelding standing quietly next to Dove. Cindy paused to gaze at him for a moment. Ben was so handsome, and he looked at ease on the gelding. *Maybe this* is *a good idea*, she decided.

Elizabeth held the mare's reins, waiting for Cindy to mount up. When she settled onto the mare's back, Dove swung her head around and sniffed at the toe of Cindy's boot. Cindy reached down to rub the dish-shaped indentation between the mare's soft eyes. "We're going to have some fun, aren't we?"

Dove snorted softly and tossed her head, making her bit jingle. Elizabeth stepped back and grinned at Cindy. "Have a nice ride, okay?"

"We will," Ben replied, then cued his gelding into a walk.

Cindy looked around the pastures as they rode up the tractor lane between two paddocks. "I've never seen Tall Oaks from this angle," she said, her head turning left and right as she drank in the view. "Things always look different from the back of a horse." She settled into the rhythm of Dove's leisurely walk. With Ben at her side, Cindy realized it wasn't just being on horseback that made her feel so happy; it was the company, too.

"It looks like you're having a good time," Ben said, keeping his leggy gelding even with the pace Cindy's mare had set.

She flashed him a broad smile. "This was very thoughtful of you," she said, patting Dove's neck. "It's the next best thing to getting back on a racehorse."

Ben dropped his chin and frowned at her, shaking his finger in a scolding gesture. "Don't push it, Cindy," he said.

"I can't help it," she replied. "That's one of the personality traits that made me such a great jockey. I never give up. I'm stubborn, remember?"

"Oh, I remember," Ben said, shaking his head wryly. "I think you and my father are in close competition for being the two most stubborn people I know."

Cindy pinched her lips together when Ben mentioned his father. "What have you heard from Dubai?"

she asked, feeling herself being lulled by the gentle rocking motion of Dove's easy walk. "Have you been able to talk to your father? How is he doing?"

Ben shook his head. "I did speak with Mother," he replied, reining his bay Arabian onto a path that wound through a small copse of trees. "She says his condition is stable, but he is still in the hospital and under close observation." As Ben spoke, his horse broke into a trot, taking several quick strides down the wood-lined trail before Ben could slow him.

Cindy squeezed her heels lightly against Dove's sides, pleased when the mare promptly picked up her pace and caught up with Ben's mount. "You do have a little fire under that gray coat, don't you, girl?" she asked softly, wondering just how well the mare could run.

They ambled along the wide dirt path for several minutes in friendly silence. Finally Ben glanced at Cindy and inhaled deeply. "We need to discuss Gratis and Champion," he said. "I've done a lot of thinking about the situation, and I feel we should do whatever we have to do to keep Champion at Tall Oaks, Cindy. Even if it means pulling Gratis from the Derby."

Cindy ground her teeth in frustration. "We need to keep Champion here *and* race Gratis," she said firmly. "Having Gratis in the race is going to bring a lot of attention to the farm, and Champion is going to provide us with some of the best bloodlines in the country." She twisted in the saddle to look at Ben. "Tall Oaks could be one of the best-known farms in the world if we manage the next couple of years correctly. I really want to do everything I can to make your farm a huge success."

Ben smiled at her. "I know you do, and with your drive and determination, you'll make a lot of things happen. But," he added, "I do think it is more important to keep Champion here than to race Gratis. Think about it. We don't even have a rider for the colt. If Brad gets Champion over to Townsend Acres, he could keep the stallion long enough that we would miss next year's breeding season. Even if we prove that his documents are in error, Townsend Acres could have a whole crop of foals by Wonder's Champion."

Cindy sank into the saddle. "I never thought of that," she said. "Do you think that's been his plan all along?"

Ben nodded slowly. "Brad is always working on some underhanded scheme," he said. "I'm sure that's what he had in mind."

"But why would he offer to let us keep Champion if we pull Gratis from the race?" Cindy asked, frowning thoughtfully.

"Because he wants to eliminate the competition," Ben said. "He doesn't think much of Christina as a jockey, so he doesn't see Star as a threat. As a filly, Image will be hard pressed to keep up with the colts. But Gratis is a wild card. Brad has seen him run, and I'm sure he'd like to make certain that Celtic Mist doesn't have to compete against our irascible bay colt."

They rode in silence for a little while before Ben spoke again. "If Celtic Mist wins the Derby, Townsend Acres won't need Champion. Brad's playing the odds, but he knows about the risks of horse racing. He's just doing everything he can to help himself come out the winner."

"How do you know so much about him?" Cindy demanded. "I've known Brad for years, but you seem to have all his angles figured out."

Ben looked amused. "I know lots of people just like

Brad," he said. "There are plenty of spoiled rich men who can't believe anyone would ever say no to them. Brad isn't so unique."

"Oh." Cindy absorbed what Ben had told her. "What about you?" she asked, suddenly curious. "You grew up around lots of money, but you don't seem ruthless. You're nothing like Brad."

Ben threw back his head and roared with laughter. The bay gelding bobbed his head in surprise, flicking his ears back at the sound, but continued steadily along the trail. "My father didn't believe in spoiling children," he said. "I earned my spending money by cleaning stalls and working alongside the other stable hands. When I went to college I had a job washing dishes in a restaurant. No one knew I was the son of a sheik, Cindy. I was never allowed to use my family name to gain favor. And I appreciate the lessons that taught me."

The trail widened, and Dove snorted and tossed her head, prancing as she tried to move ahead of Ben's bay gelding. Cindy patted the mare's neck gently and tightened the reins, but her heart sped up a little at the thought of a good hard gallop. "You seem like you'd enjoy a little run, too," she murmured to the prancing mare. But she kept Dove in check and looked at Ben again. "So Brad's really worried about Gratis," she commented thoughtfully.

Ben nodded, guiding the bay along the edge of the wide path. "Eventually he's going to figure out we don't have a jockey for the race," he cautioned Cindy. "Then we won't even have the option of pulling Gratis as a way to protect Champion."

"I could race him," Cindy said.

"You know you can't do that," Ben admonished her. "You can't ride like that anymore."

"Oh, yeah?" Cindy glanced ahead at the wide, smooth trail, then shot Ben a devilish look. "Just watch me." Before Ben could react, Cindy leaned forward in the saddle and gave Dove's flanks a firm squeeze with her heels.

With a snort of surprise, Dove lunged forward and took off at a gallop.

"Cindy, stop!" Ben called from behind her.

Cindy ignored Ben's alarmed cry. She balanced over the mare's shoulders and kneaded her fists up Dove's neck as they sped along the tree-lined path.

"You're not in the least bit dangerous, are you, Dove?" she asked, sitting easily to the mare's steady gait. Even with the mare's short strides, the feeling of galloping again was the most wonderful thing in the world.

She crouched over Dove's withers, watching the trees pass by in a rush. In the distance Cindy could see where the trail opened into a grassy meadow. Reluctantly she slowed the mare a little, but she was unable to contain a whoop of elation as they burst out of the woods and into the clearing. She circled Dove along the meadow's edge, gradually bringing the excited horse down to a trot, then a walk.

By the time they finished a circuit of the area, Ben had reached the meadow's edge. His gelding pranced in place, fighting to join Dove, but Ben restrained the horse, all the while glaring at Cindy. His eyes flashed with anger, and she cringed inwardly, knowing Ben had every right to be upset with her. But she couldn't regret her impulsive act. Galloping, even on a short-legged Arabian, had been the best thing she'd done since she'd come back to Kentucky.

She walked the breathless mare back to Ben.

"What were you doing?" Ben demanded, frowning at her.

Cindy straightened in the saddle and met his dark gaze with a determined look of her own. "I was just having a little fun," she said, patting Dove's neck. "It was great, Ben." She swung her arm around in an arc and grinned. "My shoulder feels fine," she announced.

"No more stunts like that," Ben said in a warning voice. "Otherwise Dove will be on her way to a new home."

"Lighten up," Cindy said irritably, frustrated that Ben didn't understand how much she had needed that little run.

"You can't take that kind of risk with your shoulder," Ben said, the tightness around his eyes softening a little. "You could cripple yourself for the rest of your life. Now let's head back to the barn. I've had enough excitement for one afternoon."

He turned the bay and started back along the trail, and Cindy let Dove, once again acting like a placid trail horse, amble behind the other horse.

Ben glanced behind him, a smile tugging at his

mouth. "I have to admit, that was some great riding," he said. "Just don't do it again, please. My heart can't take that kind of stress."

Cindy worked her jaw, biting back her immediate response. She knew she could race Gratis. If only Ben and the doctor could see things the way she did, they wouldn't stop her from this one last chance to ride in the greatest race of her life.

7

"Here you go, boy," Cindy said, holding a chunk of apple out to Champion. The late afternoon sun cast long shadows across the paddock. After she and Ben had returned from their ride, Elizabeth and Beckie had taken the Arabians to be groomed and turned out in their new paddocks. Ben had gone back to his office in the main house to deal with business. Before she made more calls to find a jockey for Gratis, Cindy had picked up a few apples from the feed room and went to visit her favorite stallion.

Champion took the apple, crunching it slowly. Cindy chuckled as foamy juice ran out of the horse's mouth. "You need to learn some manners," she said, rubbing his sleek nose as Champion nuzzled her pocket, searching for more treats.

She shook her head. "That was it, greedy," she said. She gazed around the farm, looking at the seemingly endless expanse of empty paddocks. She watched Elizabeth and Beckie walking the Arabians along the wide lane. Elizabeth stopped Ben's bay gelding at an empty paddock and opened the gate. After being released from his lead line, the gelding pranced a few steps into the pasture, then promptly dropped his nose and began grazing contentedly. When Cindy heard a shout of laughter, she turned her attention to Dove's paddock. She saw the mare bolt away from Beckie and gallop across the enclosure, snorting loudly as she circled the pasture with her tail flagged and her head flung high.

"I can see why you were retired from the special riding program," Cindy said to herself, laughing at the gray mare's energetic display. "You may be a small Arabian, but you have the spirit of a true Thoroughbred." After a couple of laps Dove trotted into the middle of the field and settled down to graze.

Cindy felt Champion's lips catching at her hair, and

she turned to the stallion. "That isn't hay," she said in a warning tone, shoving his nose away. "It's time to take you into the barn for dinner, anyway." She picked up the stallion's halter and lead line from where she had dropped them and slipped the headpiece over Champion's nose.

For a moment she flashed back to that terrible day so many years ago when, as a strong-willed three-year-old, Champion had broken away from her in the Whitebrook barn. He had charged down the aisle, running over Ashleigh and injuring her so badly that she had lost the baby she was expecting.

"I know it was my fault you got away and hurt Ashleigh," she told Champion, stroking his glossy neck, then smoothing her hand along his shoulder. With Ashleigh losing the baby and then deciding with Mike to sell Champion, that had been the worst time of Cindy's life.

"But now that you're back, I can't let Brad take you away." She pressed her face against his shoulder and inhaled deeply, absorbing the sweet scent of his warm coat. "Am I being too stubborn about Gratis?" she asked, her face buried in Champion's silky mane.

Champion swung his head and nudged her with his nose.

"You think I am, don't you?" she asked. "But Brad Townsend has gotten his way too many times. I can't let him order us around. Ben is going to find the papers that prove you belong here," she said, trying to reassure herself that Brad wasn't going to get away with taking Champion. "Then it won't matter if we race Gratis. Brad won't have any hold on us."

She looked around at the empty paddocks again. Tall Oaks needed Champion there to build up the farm's bloodlines, and the prestige of having another Derby winner would only help the farm's reputation.

She had thought that at Tall Oaks her life would be out of Brad Townsend's reach, but not even the al-Rihanis were invulnerable to Brad's conniving. It just wasn't fair that when things finally seemed to be going so well, Brad could find a way to shatter Cindy's dreams.

She led Champion across the paddock. Although he was still a massive, powerful animal, Champion no longer behaved like the high-strung colt who had bolted away from Cindy, starting a chain of events that still touched her. She patted his shoulder. "I know you're going to be safe," she told the horse as she opened his paddock gate. "Brad won't be able to get his hands on you. I'm sure of it."

Beckie greeted her at the barn door. "I'll put Champion away for you," she said, holding her hand out to take the stallion's lead. "Mr. al-Rihani is meeting with some fellow in your office." Beckie's face was puckered in a worried frown. "Whoever he is, the man is wearing a suit and carrying a briefcase."

Cindy silently handed the stallion's lead to the groom and turned away, hurrying toward her small office at the other end of the stallion barn.

When she reached the doorway, Ben was sitting at her desk. The visitor had pulled one of the folding chairs away from the wall and was pushing a stack of papers across the desk to Ben.

"You can see that my client, Townsend Acres, has a valid concern," the man said. "These legal documents indicate that you have no ownership in the stallion known as Wonder's Champion." He pointed at a place on the top paper. "There is the horse's Jockey Club registration number and his description. I believe that matches the stallion you currently have in your possession."

Ben looked down at the papers, then raised his head to stare at the attorney. "This only indicates that Champion is registered with the Jockey Club," he said. "And that you have some papers lacking signatures. That doesn't mean the sale of the horse was not a legal transaction."

The attorney leaned back and steepled his hands under his chin. "We're asking that you provide proof that you have legal ownership," he said. "If you can't offer us that proof, we demand that you relinquish the animal in question to its rightful owner."

Cindy inhaled sharply, forcing herself to stay quiet, although the strong words sounded as though they had the power to take Champion away.

Ben glanced at her, gave her a tight-lipped smile, then looked back at the attorney. "I will have my own attorney review these papers," he said calmly. "I know the sale was completed properly, but I don't have access to the supporting documents at this time."

"Then until you can prove your argument, we want to move the stallion to Townsend Acres."

"No," Ben said flatly.

"Mr. Townsend warned me that you would be

unreasonable," the attorney said abruptly. "You're going to force us to go to court over the matter." The man rose from his chair. He picked up his briefcase and gazed down at Ben. "I've already started the legal proceedings. We'll have a date in front of a judge within the week." He shook his head. "You could just make it easy for everyone and agree that you don't really own that stallion, Mr. al-Rihani."

Cindy clenched her jaw, struggling to keep from charging into the room and telling Brad's pompous lawyer what she thought of him.

"Go ahead and schedule a court date," Ben said, his voice low and steady. "Brad isn't going to intimidate me, and I won't be bullied by his unwarranted claim."

With a stiff nod of his head, the attorney turned away. He brushed past Cindy as though she weren't even there and headed for the barn's main doorway.

As soon as he was out of the barn, Cindy slipped into the office, her eyes locked with Ben's. "They're going to get away with it, aren't they?" she asked, sinking onto the hard chair the attorney had occupied. She was sure Ben's display of confidence had been an act for the Townsends' lawyer.

Ben looked down at the papers, slowly reading through the pages before he met Cindy's gaze again. "Brad's documents make a pretty strong argument for Champion's ownership," he said. "I will have my lawyer go over these, but without the word of Clay Townsend or my father's files, we don't have any proof that Champion was legally sold to the al-Rihanis."

Cindy dropped her chin and buried her face in her hands. "This can't be happening," she murmured. "Why can't Brad just leave us alone?"

"I'll do everything I can," Ben assured her. "But pulling Gratis would be the easiest way to resolve this whole thing, Cindy."

Cindy thought again of her brief gallop on Dove. She knew she could ride Gratis to a win in the Derby. It was just a matter of proving to Ben that her shoulder was healthy enough to handle the stress of the race.

"We can't give in to Brad," she said, feeling her stubborn streak take over. "Maybe we could track Clay Townsend down."

"I've been trying," he said. "So far my contacts in Europe haven't had any luck." He rose, picking up the papers the attorney had left for him. "I'll get these to my lawyer," he said, walking around the desk. He paused in the doorway. "But I have to tell you," he said, "it isn't looking good."

After he left, Cindy moved around to the chair behind the desk. She tried to sort out some of her own paperwork, but her mind kept drifting to Champion and to Gratis. Finally she leaned back in her chair and gazed at the ceiling. Was she being too stubborn, too unreasonable? She didn't want to lose Champion again, but she couldn't let Ben give up the chance to have Gratis win the Kentucky Derby. She heaved a sigh of frustration. It was looking as though they weren't going to be able to have both the things she wanted so much, but how could she choose one over the other?

She looked up Tommy Turner's phone number in Florida, but when she reached his answering service, she hung up without leaving a message. She quickly dialed a familiar number in Elmont, New York, and when a woman's voice answered, Cindy smiled.

"Rachel," she said, "this is Cindy." Rachel McGrady and Cindy had been roommates when Cindy first returned to New York from Dubai. A skilled jockey, Rachel had quit racing a few years before Cindy, but she and her husband, Matt McGrady, still bred race-horses and were involved in a lot of track activities.

Cindy quickly explained her dilemma.

"I know someone who might be good for that kind of colt," Rachel said, then gave Cindy a name and phone number. "When are you coming back up to New York?"

"I'll definitely be there for the running of the Belmont," Cindy said. She promised to call Rachel when she got into New York, then hung up and immediately called the jockey Rachel had told her about, trying not to get her hopes up that this rider would be the right one for Gratis.

Early the next morning Cindy was waiting at the rail when Wolf brought Gratis to the track for his work. "Let's take it easy today," she told the rider. "I just want him to do a couple of miles of easy jogging."

Wolf gave her a surprised look. "But your training schedule said he was going to do a breeze today."

"I changed my mind," Cindy said, looking steadily at Wolf. Did he have to challenge everything she said? "I believe it's your job to work the horse the way I tell you." She didn't tell Wolf she had arranged for Rachel's friend to try Gratis out the next day. That wasn't something she needed to clear with her exercise rider.

Wolf scowled at her, then swung lightly onto Gratis's back. "I'd work him the way you originally planned," he said before he started Gratis along the rail. He glanced over his shoulder as they moved away from Cindy. "You shouldn't keep second-guessing yourself," he called, then turned back to face the track.

Cindy sucked in a deep breath, stunned to silence by Wolf's comment. She wasn't second-guessing herself, was she? Changing Gratis's workout didn't mean she was acting flaky. The kid didn't know what he was talking about.

But still, Wolf's comment had struck a nerve, even if he didn't realize it. She wasn't supposed to race anymore, even though her heart knew she belonged on a racehorse, not standing beside the track holding a clipboard. She was letting the doctor, and Ben, convince her that racing again would be the worst thing she could do. More and more she was starting to think that not racing was the most awful thing she had ever experienced.

If this next jockey didn't work out, Cindy knew

what she was going to do. The challenge wouldn't be racing Gratis; it would be getting the doctor to release her to ride in the Derby, then convincing Ben that it was a good idea.

She watched Wolf urge Gratis into a jog, keeping a close eye on the colt. When she saw his ears flick as he reached the curve in the oval, she knew what was going to happen, and Gratis didn't disappoint her.

The colt stopped abruptly and reared, lashing at the air with his powerful front legs. Cindy watched Wolf lean forward on Gratis's shoulders, staying with the horse as he lunged forward. Before Gratis could kick with his back legs, Wolf had straightened in the saddle and brought the horse's head to the side. With his nose at his shoulder, Gratis couldn't buck. He minced sideways for several steps, trying to get his head loose so that he could take off, but Wolf kept him under control.

Cindy stifled a chuckle. She'd done the same thing many times when a horse tried to unseat her. She nodded thoughtfully. Wolf seemed to think he was the only rider around who could outthink Gratis, but Cindy could read the colt just as well as he could. And on top of that, she was qualified to race.

Gratis pranced, stiff-legged, still testing Wolf, but finally Wolf straightened the colt out and moved him along the back stretch of the track. After tossing his head a few times, the colt settled down into a smooth jog, not showing a hint that he had ever given a thought to dumping his rider.

Cindy folded her arms across her chest. This was almost like when she'd been trying to make it on her own as a young jockey in New York. If no one would give her a chance, she'd have to make it happen herself.

She reassured herself that Ben would find a way to keep Champion. He wouldn't let Brad force them into relinquishing the stallion. And she would find a way to race Gratis in the Derby. She understood how to compete in that kind of high-pressure, high-stakes race, and she knew that with her on his back, the colt stood a good chance of winning.

8

"If you think you're going to find someone to race that horse in the Kentucky Derby, you're out of your mind," Chuck Jackson said, dusting the dirt from Tall Oaks' practice track off his jeans. Gratis was galloping along the rail, riderless. Cindy watched Wolf duck under the rail, then turned away, leaving the exercise rider to catch the running horse.

"Can't you give him one more try?" she asked Chuck, giving the irate jockey a pleading look. Chuck had managed to stay on the colt longer than any of the other jockeys who had tried him out, but after being thrown twice, the man had walked off the track, shaking his head.

"Not a chance," Chuck said, frowning toward Gratis, who had slowed to a canter as he neared Wolf. "I can ride just about anything, but that colt has some big problems, Ms. McLean. Maybe if I had some time to work with him, I'd try him in a couple of smaller races, but I'm not going to risk my professional reputation by taking that colt into the Derby. With the way he acts, someone could get killed during the race, and I certainly don't want it to be me."

Cindy nodded in understanding. "Thanks for giving him a tryout, anyway," she said, attempting to hide her deep disappointment. Chuck had all the credentials and experience she wanted in a jockey, and now her hopes had been crushed once again.

"I was coming down to Lexington anyway," Chuck said. "So it wasn't a problem when Rachel asked if I would check out your colt as a favor to Matt and her. I'm sorry it didn't work out." He glanced toward the track. "I would love to race in the Derby, but not on him."

Cindy looked over to where Wolf was leading Gratis, who was snorting and prancing at the end of his lead, toward them.

As Chuck walked away, Ben came out of the house and headed for the track.

"Another Gratis disaster, I take it?" he asked when he reached Cindy.

She nodded, smiling gamely. "There's still me," she said, avoiding Ben's gaze. "I could handle him, you know."

"I'm sure you could if your shoulder weren't an issue," Ben said. "But we both know you're not going to risk taking that colt on. We need to give up our plan for racing him in the Derby, Cindy."

"Just let me get on him once," Cindy persisted. "You'll see just how well I can manage his little tantrums, and then we'll be Derby-bound."

But even as she was speaking, Ben was shaking his head in a definite no. "Brad and his attorney are coming by in a while to review the papers on Champion," he said. "After you have Wolf put the colt up, I need you to come to the house so we can go over the information my attorney gave me."

"I'll be up in a few minutes," Cindy said. Ben walked away, and Cindy turned to the track. Wolf

103

brought Gratis to a stop near the rail. He was looking at Cindy through narrowed eyes.

Cindy ignored Wolf, giving Gratis's nose a fond pet. The colt nuzzled her hand, then tried to nip her fingers playfully. "No!" she said sharply, giving his mouth a flick with her fingers. Gratis snorted and tossed his head a little, then shoved his nose toward her again.

"Go ahead and put him in his turnout after you've groomed him," she told Wolf. "Then you can see if Elizabeth has some tack that needs cleaning."

"That's my kind of job," Wolf said, curling his lip.

Cindy bristled. "I spent a lot of time cleaning tack even when I was a jockey," she said. "It's part of the business. If you're too good—"

Wolf cut her short with an abrupt wave. "I didn't say I was too good," he snapped. "I just don't know why you won't let me do what I do best."

"And what is that, besides tell everyone just how great you are?" Cindy asked, propping her hands on her hips.

"I can ride Gratis better than any of your highly skilled jockeys," Wolf retorted. He didn't give Cindy a chance to respond, but instead turned and led Gratis toward the barn.

Cindy watched him stalk away. After a few minutes she walked back to the barn. Once in her office she slumped into her chair, at a loss as to what she should do.

"Cindy?"

She looked up to see Elizabeth standing in the doorway. "I need to run to Lexington, and I thought I'd take Beckie with me. Is that all right?"

Cindy smiled at her assistant. "Sure," she said. "While you're there, will you stop by the feed store and pick up a bag of vitamin supplement for Gratis?"

"Sure," Elizabeth said. "Is there anything else you need?"

"That's it," Cindy replied. "I'll see you later."

After Elizabeth left, Cindy looked through her list of jockeys, searching without hope for someone else who might be able to race Gratis. When the phone rang, she picked it up. "Tall Oaks," she said absently.

"Cindy, I need you up at the house right now." Ben's voice sounded strained.

Cindy sat up straight. "I'll be right there," she said.

She left the barn and hurried up toward the mansion, her stomach knotted with stress. When she saw Brad's car parked in the paved drive, she slowed, knowing with a dreadful certainty that whatever was going on at the house meant bad news for Champion.

She climbed up the steps and hesitated at the double doors, debating whether to knock or simply walk into the house. Finally she took a deep breath and opened the door. The foyer was almost as big as her entire cottage, and Cindy felt small standing in the spacious entry. She looked around the interior, postponing the moment when she would have to face Brad. Finally she looked from the tall potted plants, the artwork hanging from the walls, and the gleaming expanse of wood floor to the open doorway of Ben's office. She could see Ben, Brad, and Brad's haughty attorney standing in the middle of the room, deep in discussion. Cindy took a deep breath, then strode purposefully into the office.

"We can have a trailer here in an hour," Brad was saying when she entered the room. "Unless you want to go through the embarrassment of a court proceeding, you'll give up the stallion."

"Not until I've spoken with my father, or yours," Ben said in a cold voice. "I find it very questionable that you are pushing this action at a time when neither of them is available to confirm your claim."

"This has been an issue for Townsend Acres for years," Brad said. "There was nothing we could do until Champion was back in the United States. Now that he's here, we want him back."

A sudden thought made Cindy feel giddy with relief, and she stepped closer, eager to shut Brad down once and for all. "What about the interest Ashleigh sold to the sheik?" she interjected loudly. It might take months to prove that the al-Rihanis legally owned Champion, but if they were even half owners because of Ashleigh's sale of her interest in the stallion, it would be easier to keep him at Tall Oaks.

The three men turned to look at her. The attorney looked shocked, Ben looked hopeful, but Brad merely smirked at her. "Because of the tragic situation at the time, Ashleigh signed her interest over to my father, and he paid her the money she was due. She released her interest in the stallion to Townsend Acres before the al-Rihanis moved the stallion out of the country."

Cindy felt her heart sink, and Ben's expression darkened.

"I still need to clear things with my lawyer," he said to Brad and the attorney. "You'll have to wait. A few more days won't make any difference, will they?"

The attorney stood rigid, a sheaf of papers clutched in one hand. "The Townsends' concern is that you might try to move the horse prior to the issue being resolved. We don't want you sending him back to the United Arab Emirates. That would create a very difficult situation."

"I don't intend to take him out of the country," Ben said, irritation clear in his voice. "What does Townsend Acres plan to do if you get him?" he asked, his voice growing quiet.

Cindy knew the extreme calm in Ben's voice was his way of covering up the anger he felt over the situation. She admired his ability to control himself. She, on the other hand, always seemed to speak before considering the consequences of what she was saying.

"What Townsend Acres does with the stallion is none of your business," the attorney replied in an equally level tone. "You're going to have to give up the

108

horse sooner or later. Why not just make it simpler for everyone?"

"Because the Townsends are wrong on this," Ben said, smiling thinly. "Now, I'll ask you two to leave so I can take care of my own business."

"You can't keep postponing this," Brad said in a warning tone, then turned and strode past Cindy, not even giving her so much as a glance. His attorney laid the bundle of pages on Ben's desk. "You'll want to share those with your legal advisor," he said, then followed Brad out of the house.

After they heard the door shut, Ben sank down onto his chair and gazed across the desk at Cindy. "It doesn't look good at all," he said. "The papers they've provided are in order, and it looks like Champion is going to Townsend Acres."

"Then we'll give up racing Gratis," Cindy said, hating the thought of giving in to Brad's demands.

But Ben shook his head slowly. "We waited too long," he said. "Brad knows we don't have a jockey for Gratis. He's withdrawn that offer."

Cindy stood frozen, staring at Ben. She had been so stubborn, wanting to have everything. And now she was going to lose Champion *and* not be able to offer Ben the chance to stand in the winner's circle with Gratis after the Derby. "I'm sorry, Ben," she said softly.

Ben looked down at the pile of papers on his desk. "I need to take these into town," he said. "Maybe my lawyer can find something wrong in these new documents, something that will help us keep Champion."

"I'll be at the barn if you need me," Cindy said sadly. She left, any hope she'd had that everything would turn out all right slipping away. She knew Ben was very worried about his father, and she had only added to his stress by pushing the fight with Brad even after he had offered them a way of keeping Champion.

By the time she reached the barn Ben was heading down the drive in his big red pickup. Cindy smiled. Rather than driving a sleek European sports car the way Brad Townsend did, the farm owner drove an American-made truck, as though he'd been driving the back roads of Kentucky all his life.

Before she went into the barn, Cindy walked over to Champion's turnout. The stallion was standing quietly in his paddock, his head relaxed and his feet splayed as he dozed in the late morning sun. Cindy felt like crying.

The big chestnut looked so contented and peaceful. She didn't know what would happen to him if he ended up at Townsend Acres, but she knew he wouldn't be treated with the love and affection that the al-Rihanis had shown him in Dubai or that he enjoyed at Tall Oaks.

"Hey, Cindy!"

When she looked up to see Christina striding toward the paddock rail, Cindy turned away from Champion and forced herself to put on a bright smile. Christina joined her at the paddock and leaned her forearms on the top of the fence. She gazed at Champion, then glanced at Cindy.

"I was so young when he left that I really don't remember much about him," she said. "Mom says Champion was always high-strung and hard to handle, but that you were better than anyone else with him."

Cindy let her gaze return to the paddock, where Champion, still powerful-looking and majestic, basked contentedly. "He was a handful," she agreed. "But you're a much better jockey than I ever dreamed of being, Chris. Look how far you've come in such a short time."

Christina shrugged modestly. "I've been lucky," she said. "I've been given lots of great chances, and things have worked out right for me." She turned her attention from Champion to Cindy. "I've been doing a lot of thinking," she said.

"About what?" Cindy asked, curious.

"I made a decision." Christina swallowed hard. "I want to race Gratis in the Derby."

Cindy gaped at Christina, stunned to realize the offer was sincere, that Christina was dead serious about riding the unruly colt. She stared at Christina, unable to speak. That Christina had even considered riding Gratis in the first place had struck Cindy as very generous, but now Christina's sincere offer to race the colt was overwhelming. Cindy swallowed around a lump that had formed in her throat, and she forced herself to shake her head.

"I can't let you do that," Cindy finally responded. "We talked about you and Star, Chris. You've gone through too much together not to have this shot at the Triple Crown. I really appreciate the offer, but you're going to ride Star. Gratis is my problem, not yours."

Christina glanced away for a moment. When she

looked back at Cindy, her expression was determined. "It wouldn't be hard to get someone else to ride Star," she said. "I know you've been doing everything you can to find a rider for Gratis, and I know I could race him. I think I'm the last chance you have for him, Cindy. You'd better let me do this."

Cindy wavered, torn by the temptation that Christina was offering. With Christina in the saddle, Gratis would run well, and Cindy's worries about the race would be ended. She might not be able to stop Brad from taking Champion, but she could at least give Ben this. She opened her mouth, then clamped it shut.

She couldn't let Christina give up what she had worked so hard for. Slowly Cindy shook her head. "No," she said firmly. "You're going to ride Star and do well. Gratis is my problem, Chris, not yours."

Christina exhaled, and Cindy was sure she heard a whisper of relief in the sigh.

"If you change your mind, the offer still stands," Christina said.

Cindy reached over and gave the young jockey a quick hug. "Thank you, Chris," she said, close to tears over the generosity of Christina's offer. She looked away for a few seconds, not wanting to show how deeply touched she was over Christina's willingness to sacrifice her shot at Triple Crown glory to help a friend. When she looked back, she had her emotions reined in. "We'll get things figured out with Gratis, honest."

After Christina left, Cindy turned back to watch Champion doze. She swallowed a lump of tears that had formed in her throat, not sure if she felt like crying because of the sacrifice Christina had been willing to make, the chance of losing Champion again, or her own inability to get Gratis on the track herself. *It's probably a combination of all three*, she told herself, turning away from the paddock to return to the barn.

The barn was quiet when Cindy walked inside and headed for her office. Elizabeth and Beckie were still running errands, but she saw Wolf, sitting near the tack room, a pile of leather at his feet. He was rubbing saddle soap into a headstall, but when Cindy walked by, he glanced up and gave her a cold look. Cindy stopped in front of him.

"You know I can ride Gratis better than anyone else, except maybe Christina Reese," Wolf said, setting the headstall down. "But you won't even let me try."

Cindy felt her jaw go slack. "Christina is a fully licensed jockey," she pointed out. "You haven't even been exercise-riding for a year."

"But Gratis and I understand each other," Wolf countered. He stood up and stared evenly at Cindy. "Your problem is that you think you should be the one to race him, and no one else will do. You're just mad because you're a has-been jockey. That's why you won't even give me a chance."

"That's *it!*" Cindy exploded. "I've had enough of you!" She pointed her finger at Wolf and glared back at him. "You're fired," she said. "I'll make sure your final paycheck is sent to your home address, but you can leave now."

"You can't fire me!" Wolf exclaimed. "You don't have anyone else who can handle Gratis."

"It doesn't matter," Cindy said. "Gratis isn't going to be racing in the Derby, so I have plenty of time to find a new exercise rider for his four-year-old season."

Wolf glared at her for a few seconds, then shrugged. "That's just fine by me," he said, dropping the can of saddle soap. It hit the floor on its side and rolled away, bumping against the wall before it stopped. Cindy looked from the can of soap to Wolf, then pointed at the open barn door. "Now," she said, and Wolf stormed from the building, his jaw clenched and his hands fisted.

Cindy sank onto the chair where he had been cleaning tack and buried her face in her hands. She sat there for a moment, trying to sort out her feelings, but there was too much going around in her head to make any sense. There was only one thing that would make her feel better and give her a sense of having some control of her life. She needed to go for a ride. She thought about Dove, but as much as she had enjoyed riding the little gray mare, Dove wasn't a racehorse. Cindy needed to get back on a Thoroughbred and prove, at least to herself, that she could handle one of the powerful horses. And she knew which horse she needed to ride. She dug through the tack scattered at her feet until she found Gratis's halter. Then she rose, halter in hand, and headed toward the colt's turnout.

9

"Hold still and I'll have you saddled and ready to go in a minute," Cindy told Gratis as the bay colt pawed the ground impatiently. He tossed his head, tugging at the crossties that held him in the middle of the barn aisle. Cindy patted his shoulder. "You want to get out as much as I do, don't you?" she murmured as Gratis snorted loudly, dancing his hindquarters back and forth.

Cindy settled the saddle onto his back and quickly fastened the girth, then slipped the colt's headstall into place. Gratis eagerly grabbed the bit, nudging Cindy's arm as she buckled the throatlatch.

"Just another minute," she said with a laugh as she

117

led the antsy colt from the barn. She felt as eager as he seemed. In a moment she was on his back. The energy Gratis radiated seemed to hum right through the reins. The feeling brought back the tense excitement Cindy always felt when she mounted up in the viewing paddock just before a big race.

Underneath her, Gratis felt as though he was ready to burst from the starting gate and fly down the track. Cindy collected the reins, holding the colt still. "We're going for a hack, not a race," she reminded the fiery colt, gently patting his sleek, muscular neck. Gratis pranced in place, snorting and blowing as he tossed his head and danced his hindquarters around, trying to move forward.

When she headed him up the tractor lane between the paddocks, Gratis strained against the hold Cindy had on him. "You're really wired, aren't you?" she asked, using both legs and arms to keep the powerful colt in check. She wiggled her shoulder a little, pleased at how strong it felt in spite of fighting to keep Gratis at a brisk walk when she knew all he wanted to do was explode into a furious gallop.

She watched Gratis's head closely, steeling herself

for the energetic colt to pull one of his tricks. But although he was high-strung and eager to go, the horse didn't show any signs of wanting to unload his rider. Cindy rubbed his neck gently. "You would be good if I rode you on the track, wouldn't you?"

As they neared the end of the tractor lane, Cindy could see the wooded trail she and Ben had been on, which started just beyond the tidy rows of fenced paddocks. She turned Gratis in that direction, and the colt flicked his ears back as though questioning where they were going.

"We're just going to take a little trail ride," she told him. Gratis allowed her to guide him away from the open spaces of the fenced fields, closer to the tree-lined path.

"So far so good," she told the horse as they reached the head of the trail. Suddenly Gratis reared a little, clearly on edge about starting down the strange-looking route. Tall trees shaded the path. Patches of sunlight filtered between the broad leaves of the oak and maple trees, and the slight movement of the leaves caused the sunny spots to move on the ground.

The colt snorted loudly and sidled away from the

beginning of the trail, trying to wheel around and head back toward the open paddocks and the tractor lane. Cindy quickly brought his head around so that he was facing the trail again. "This isn't something to be afraid of," she scolded him. "Just calm down and trust me. Once you get going, you're going to enjoy this. It'll be a good break from the track."

Gratis flicked his ears back, listening, and gradually settled down. He faced the opening in the woods, and Cindy gave him enough loose rein that he could drop his nose close to the ground. Gratis inhaled loudly, then raised his head and sniffed the air.

"It's fine, boy," Cindy said in a reassuring tone. "Nothing here is going to hurt you, I promise."

Finally Gratis took a cautious step onto the trail. "Good boy," Cindy said, stroking his neck. "The ground didn't swallow you up or anything, did it?" Gratis took another hesitant step, then a third, and at long last they were on the trail. His confidence grew as Gratis got used to the unusual sounds of the woods. He swiveled his ears in every direction, taking in the whisper of the breeze rustling the leaves, the different noises the ground underfoot made as he walked, the chattering of squirrels and the cheery songs of the birds high overhead.

When he paused to sniff at a bush growing close to the trail, Cindy laughed. "I'm sure that doesn't smell like anything you've ever eaten," she said, urging the curious horse forward. The farther they moved down the trail, the more sure of himself Gratis became. Soon he was prancing again, eager to pick up his speed. When he gave a hard toss of his head, Cindy felt a slight pull in her shoulder. Gratis yanked his head again, harder this time, and the pull Cindy had felt began to hurt. She carefully increased her grip on the reins, testing the strength of her shoulder. It didn't feel bad, just uncomfortable, and she settled deeply in the saddle, focusing her attention on the high-strung Thoroughbred. *I need to start exercising more,* she told herself. *That feeling isn't my injury; it's just my out-of-shape muscles.*

Cindy released a breath she hadn't realized she was holding. Gratis swiveled his ears back at the sound, and she patted his shoulder. "I guess we should have tried our first ride in one of the paddocks," she told him, still alert to any cues the colt might give that would indicate he planned to do something to unseat her. She began to wish she hadn't been so impulsive as to take the colt out all alone. But, she reminded herself, no one would have agreed to let her take him out at all if she'd told anyone at the farm what she was doing.

Gratis moved ahead steadily, giving a strong tug on the reins every few minutes as if to check on the grip Cindy had on him. Finally she allowed him to speed up to a long-strided trot. Cindy posted easily to the colt's gait and felt herself release a little of the tension that had knotted up her neck and shoulders.

"We're going to be great, aren't we?" she asked Gratis in a soothing voice. "We could be an impressive team on the track. I know it."

The trail widened and straightened out, and Gratis's ears snapped forward at the long stretch of smooth dirt ahead of them. Cindy felt him suddenly tense, and she put her weight firmly on his back, prepared for a bolt or worse. Gratis jerked his head forward, yanking on the reins, and Cindy felt something in her shoulder pop.

She gasped at the pain that shot down her arm, but forced herself to keep a tight hold on the reins. Gratis pranced, fighting the restraining pull on his mouth. Every toss of his head sent another intense jolt down

Cindy's arm. More than ever, she wished she hadn't taken Gratis out riding alone.

From a nearby tree, a squirrel began chattering loudly, scolding at them in a loud voice. Gratis gave a startled snort and jumped sideways, wrenching Cindy's already aching shoulder.

"Settle down," she snapped at the colt, who scampered ahead several strides before she could bring him back down to a mincing walk. For a few more minutes Gratis was somewhat agreeable, but each time he tugged at the reins, Cindy's arm suffered. She sighed, embarrassed and disappointed. "I guess I just proved everyone right," she muttered, disgusted with herself. "All I've managed to do is hurt my shoulder again. I'll never be getting back on a racetrack. And if Ben finds out I took you out, he'll get rid of the saddle horses. He only got them so he could go riding with me."

Stifling her sadness, she rubbed Gratis's red-brown neck. "You've proven to me that I can't do it, boy," she said. "I can't ever race again."

Gratis dragged at the reins again, shoving his nose toward an interesting bush. Cindy was barely able to bring his head back in line. The pain in her shoulder had settled into an intense ache, made worse every time Gratis challenged her.

"I think we'd better get back to the barn," she said sadly. She started to turn the colt, who took a step off the trail and jumped in surprise at the snapping and rustling of the underbrush. The pain Cindy felt sent a rush of dizziness to her head, and for a terrifying moment things started to go black around her.

She blinked rapidly, forcing the darkness back, and pulled at Gratis's head as best she could. But her throbbing shoulder didn't have the strength to fight the colt's power. Gratis took one more step into the bushes, and suddenly there was a blur of movement underfoot and the sound of wings flapping frantically as a startled quail burst from its hiding place in the woods.

Gratis threw his head up, nearly knocking Cindy into a tree trunk. His head narrowly missed hitting a large branch as he spun around, lunging out of the woods and back onto the trail. Cindy was barely able to stay in the saddle, let alone control the direction the colt was taking. She hauled his nose around to her foot with her good hand and they spun in circles for a minute while Gratis tried with all his strength to tear free.

Finally he calmed down. With a gasp of relief Cindy allowed him a little slack, and the colt brought his head away from his side. He took another step sideways, almost into the underbrush again, and for the second time the quail shot out of the brush, practically under Gratis's stamping feet. The second assault was too much for the agitated colt.

With a terror-filled snort he ripped the reins from Cindy's hands and broke into a gallop, racing blindly down the trail.

10

Gratis flew along the trail at a dead run, his head high and his mane slapping Cindy's face. She leaned forward, struggling just to stay on the racing colt's back as he galloped uncontrollably down the path. Her shoulder throbbed with pain as she gripped Gratis's mane, clinging helplessly to his neck as he continued his rough gallop. The trees seemed to crowd in on them, making the horse's already fast pace seem even faster.

Don't you dare pass out, Cindy ordered herself, feeling the dizzying darkness start to close in again. She fought against it, trying to keep herself from losing consciousness.

Memories of wrecks on the track filled her mind: the

sound of thundering hooves as she toppled from a racing Thoroughbred's back, tumbling over and over when she hit the ground, never knowing if one of the other horses was going to run her over. She would not let herself fall off Gratis. The horse was running away from Tall Oaks; if she did fall, he would almost certainly run himself into an injury, and it could be hours before anyone from the farm figured out where she and Gratis might be.

She forced herself to ignore the agony in her shoulder, focusing on Gratis's movement and her balance. After what felt like an eternity she pushed herself up, sitting straight in the saddle, and caught the reins. She took a deep breath and hauled back on them with all the strength she had. Pain tore through her shoulder, and she cried out, trying not to lose her grip on the reins.

Gratis threw his head high, making his bumpy gallop even rougher, and Cindy let the reins slip from her grasp and struggled to keep her seat on the madly running Thoroughbred.

This can't be happening, Cindy told herself. "Gratis," she called. "Easy, boy, easy."

But the panicked colt didn't seem to hear her. His breathing sounded loud and harsh as he charged farther away from the farm, trying to escape the bird that had frightened him. Cindy sucked in a deep breath and tried to grab the reins again, but the pain in her shoulder was so bad, she let go immediately. Every pound of Gratis's hooves on the hard-packed trail sent another jolt of agony through her shoulder, and Cindy was sure she was going to fall from the colt's back. But even as she thought about falling, an even greater worry overtook her. Galloping on the hard-packed ground must be doing terrible damage to the Thoroughbred's delicate leg bones. She felt sick at the thought of Gratis being crippled because of her mistake.

She leaned forward, trying not to think about hitting the hard ground as she struggled to come up with a way to bring the racing colt under control.

Gratis finally started to slow, then veered to the side of the trail. Cindy exhaled and started to sit up again, sure she could continue to slow him down. But a branch slapped the colt's shoulder, and he surged ahead as though he had been stung by a jockey's whip.

Low branches caught at Cindy's head and shoulders, nearly tearing her from the colt's back. She hung on desperately, still trying to use her good arm to bring the terrified horse under control. But Gratis ignored the pressure on the bit. He was a trained racehorse, and the pulling only gave him a point to balance against as he ran.

With a groan of frustration, Cindy released the reins, hoping Gratis's conditioning would get him to respond to the lack of pressure. But the colt ran blindly, too distraught to do anything but instinctively race ahead on the straight stretch.

A sweeping maple branch caught the side of Cindy's head, bringing tears to her eyes. She felt a trickle of warm blood flow down the side of her face. Another branch whacked her bad shoulder, and she gasped as intense pain coursed through her body. She ducked as they neared a low-hanging limb. The bark scraped across her back as they continued their head-long flight. *One more like that and I'll be lucky to only get knocked off,* she thought grimly, leaning her weight to the right. In response to his rider's shift, Gratis edged back to the middle of the trail, away from the trees, but he still continued on his panicked flight.

Cindy peered around the colt's head, trying to see where they were on the trail. The clearing she had galloped Dove into couldn't be far away, and she wondered what the colt would do when he reached the end of the trail. In his agitated state, he might run straight across the little meadow and crash into the trees on the far side. At the speed Gratis was going, they would both be badly injured.

"Easy, boy," she called, but Gratis raced on, his ears flattened to his head as he thundered up the path. In her mind, Cindy heard shouting and other hoofbeats. She was startled, then realized she must be remembering some of the more spectacular crashes she'd experienced on the racetrack. *I will* not *fall*, she told herself firmly, knowing that if the colt tripped on a root or brushed against another branch, she would certainly come off. But Gratis stayed to the middle of the trail, and somehow she managed to cling to his back, trying once again to slow the frightened horse by taking up the reins.

She could see sweat darkening his coat, and foam

flew from his mouth as he continued to run. *He has to be getting tired*, she told herself, but she knew the conditioning work she'd had Wolf put him through had helped the Thoroughbred stay in excellent shape. Gratis could run for a long time unless something got in his way. And Cindy knew from experience that a runaway horse would run itself to death, or blindly into a solid object, before it would stop on its own.

She was startled by a flash of movement at the corner of her eye, and she glanced quickly to her side to see Wolf galloping beside them. He was riding bareback on Ben's bay gelding. She wondered how it was possible that the Arabian could keep up with Gratis. Then she realized that while the Thoroughbred was moving at a fast pace, Gratis wasn't galloping as hard as he would in the controlled setting of the racetrack.

Wolf moved the gelding close and leaned over, catching Gratis's reins in his left hand. Cindy nearly sobbed with relief at the thought that the colt was finally going to slow down. She clung to Gratis's back and watched the young rider brace himself on the bay's sleek back, then pull the colt's head to the side. For a moment she was sure that Wolf would be pulled from the bay's back or that Gratis would swerve into the Arabian and they would all go down in a nightmarish tangle.

At the tug on the reins, Gratis tried to jerk his head free again, but to Cindy's relief Wolf was ready for the pull. He let the reins slide through his hand as Gratis tossed his head. Wolf then gave another firm yank, causing Gratis to falter a little. The jolt nearly unseated Cindy. She scrambled to keep her balance, trying to cling to the colt's back as more dizzying pain swept through her.

"Hang on!" Wolf yelled at her.

Cindy felt her irritation at Wolf start to well up, overcoming her pain, but she grimly realized she wasn't in any position to argue while she was helplessly hanging on to an out-of-control racehorse. She gritted her teeth and tangled her fingers in Gratis's mane, putting all her energy into staying on the colt's back.

"Knock it off, you meathead!" she heard Wolf yell at the frightened colt. Gratis flicked his ears in response to the rider's voice, and Cindy felt his headlong gallop slow almost imperceptibly. Wolf pulled harder at the reins, and Gratis dropped his pace a little more. Cindy looked ahead to see that they had almost reached the clearing. As they galloped into the meadow Wolf used the Arabian to crowd Gratis, getting the colt to circle the grassy area. By the time they completed a round of the clearing, Wolf had gradually brought the runaway horse under control.

Cindy groaned in pain as they bounced to a stop. She wanted to slide from Gratis's back, but the ground seemed too far away, so instead she sat quietly, relieved that her wild ride was over and sick about the disaster she had nearly created by taking Gratis out.

"Are you okay?" Wolf asked, the gelding blowing heavily as the young rider moved the horses into a calming walk, continuing to circle the meadow at a leisurely pace.

"My shoulder," Cindy gasped, barely able to get the words out.

"I don't know why you thought you could handle Gratis," Wolf said, shaking his head in disgust.

Cindy bit back the sharp words that wanted to leap off her tongue. Wolf had just saved both her and Gratis after she had fired him in a fit of temper. And as hard as it was to admit it, even to herself, he was right. She'd had no business taking the colt out the way she had.

"Just hang on," Wolf said, heading the horses back toward the trail. "I'll pony you back to the barn."

Since there was nothing else she could do, Cindy sat silently on Gratis's back, letting Wolf lead them back along the trail. When they neared the spot where the quail had spooked Gratis, the colt snorted loudly and began prancing. Cindy tightened her grip on his mane, and Wolf forced the colt to keep pace with the slower-moving Arabian. Finally they cleared the woods, and Cindy heaved another sigh of relief. The open paddocks and the distant barns looked wonderful. For a time, as Gratis had carried her closer to disaster, Cindy had begun to wonder if she would ever see Tall Oaks again.

"Thank you," she murmured to Wolf as they walked along the tractor lane.

"I couldn't let you run away with my favorite racehorse," the exercise rider said nonchalantly. When they neared the barns he brought the horses to a stop. Cindy slid from Gratis's back, groaning with pain as she wrenched her shoulder in the dismount.

"I'll put him up for you," Wolf said as he jumped from the gelding's back. He gave Cindy a superior look. "And I won't make you pay me extra, even though I don't work here anymore."

Cindy cringed. She knew she should apologize and give Wolf back his job, but she didn't know how to say it. She tried to smile, but she could tell by the way her face felt that the expression was more of a grimace. Rather than trying to talk to the young man, she nodded, then, without saying a word, slowly made her way to the cottage.

Once inside, she collapsed on the sofa, her legs trembling too much to carry her across the room to the telephone. She sat shaking with relief and exhaustion for several minutes before she dared to stand up again. Finally she made her way to the phone and quickly called the doctor.

"I'll meet you at the hospital," Dr. Klein said when she described the pain.

Cindy picked up her purse, but the thought of driving herself into Lexington was too much for her. She started across the room again to call Whisperwood. Maybe Samantha or Tor could take her to the doctor.

But a knock on the door made her set the telephone down. When she opened the door, Wolf was standing there, looking uncomfortable.

"I cooled Gratis out and put him in his stall," he said. "He's pretty well calmed down, but I didn't think you'd want him in his turnout after getting so worked up with his gallop through the woods. He might run himself through a fence or something."

"Thank you," Cindy said, aware that Wolf had done exactly what she would have told him to do if her head had been clear. What had she been *thinking*, firing him? She could learn a thing or two from Ben about using self-control when it came to running a business.

Wolf pointed at her arm, which hung limp at her side. "Do you need a ride to the doctor's office?" he asked, then gave her a hard look. "I was leaving anyway, remember?"

"I can take myself," Cindy started to say, but she caught herself. *Tell him you're sorry,* she thought. *You owe him at least that much.* But when she opened her mouth, the apology stuck in her throat. "If it isn't too much trouble, you could drop me off at the hospital," she said.

"My car's right outside," Wolf said, turning away. Cindy picked up her purse and followed Wolf to his battered sedan.

They made the drive into Lexington in silence. Cindy was at a complete loss for words, wondering how she'd ever gotten herself into such a difficult situation. *You're an adult*, she scolded herself. *You're supposed to think before you act.* But she obviously hadn't been thinking clearly that day.

Wolf pulled up at the wide doors of the emergency entrance and helped Cindy from the car.

"Thank you," she said before she walked through the door.

"I'll go call Mr. al-Rihani," Wolf told her. "He's got to be wondering where you are."

Cindy nodded and turned away. *He'll probably fire me when he hears about my little adventure*, she thought glumly as she walked up to the reception desk. *And it won't be any less than I deserve.*

11

"I can't believe I'm back here," Cindy said, looking around the white walls of the hospital room.

After having X rays and a careful examination in the emergency room, Cindy had been given a long lecture by Dr. Klein. She had been relieved to learn that she wouldn't need additional surgery.

"But we will need to immobilize your arm for several weeks," Dr. Klein had informed her. The doctor had pointed his finger at Cindy and given her a stern look. "And there will be no more wild rides, right?"

Cindy had nodded compliantly. "I won't ever do that again," she said, and meant it sincerely. The close call with Gratis had made her realize, with absolute finality, that she could not handle the physical stress of controlling a racehorse.

Now her arm was immobilized with a sturdy sling, her pain subdued by medication the doctor had prescribed. The bandage on her face made the deep scratch from the branch seem worse than it felt, but the doctor had been worried about a possible concussion. Her frantic ride on Gratis seemed like a distant dream at the moment.

Ben sat beside the bed, shaking his head. "I can't believe you took that colt on the trails," he said, giving her a disapproving look. "You could have been badly hurt, Cindy."

She tried to smile bravely, but she felt like crying, so instead she looked down at her bandaged arm and blinked back tears. "I was able to stay on because I'm a good rider, Ben," she said quietly.

Ben released an exasperated sigh. "I *know* you're a good rider," he said. "I've watched you race, remember? But you knew better than to take a high-strung racehorse out like that."

Cindy nodded, still unable to meet the eyes of the man sitting beside her. "I overestimated myself," she admitted. Finally she glanced up at him from under her lashes. "Are you going to fire me?" she asked in a small voice.

At that, Ben laughed. "No, I'm not going to fire you. I'm not even going to sell Dove. But I do hope you've learned your lesson. I was so afraid when Wolf called to let me know he'd brought you to the hospital. Don't you ever put me through that kind of fright again."

Cindy nodded in agreement. "I've definitely learned my lesson the hard way," she said. "Thank goodness the vet says there's no damage to Gratis's legs. I don't know how I'd live with myself if I'd ruined that horse." She sighed and looked up at Ben. "I'm so sorry I worried you. I wouldn't blame you for being mad at me."

Ben gave her good arm a gentle pat. "I know," he said. "But I can't be mad at you for being the kind of person you are." He paused, then smiled at her. "You remind me a lot of Wolf, you know."

Cindy stared at him, shocked. "I what?" she gasped.

Ben nodded. "You're sure of yourself, determined, focused. All those things that helped you make it at the track are the same things that I've seen in Wolf." He glanced at his watch. "I have to go make some phone calls," he said. "Brad's lawyer has been directed to speak only to my attorney, so they won't be hounding us personally anymore." He sighed. "It still looks as though we'll be losing Champion."

Cindy nodded. Everything seemed to be going wrong, so it was no surprise that Brad was going to win the fight for the stallion's ownership. The setbacks meant it could be years before Tall Oaks regained its reputation in the Thoroughbred world as a breeder of top racehorses. "And now we definitely don't have a rider for Gratis," she said. "I'm sorry, Ben."

Ben leaned over and gave her a soft kiss on the cheek. "I'm quite upset that you risked yourself the way you did," he said. "But still, that's the Cindy I've always admired, stubborn and determined." He rose and headed for the door, then glanced back, a smile softening his face. "You have guts, Cindy, and I respect that."

Cindy lay back against the pillows the nurse had tucked behind her head and gazed up at the ceiling. At least Ben still respected her. That was a good thing. She thought about what he had said about Wolf reminding him of her, and she closed her eyes. Maybe that was why the kid irritated her so much. He still had the chance to make it on the track, while she had been forced to leave that part of the Thoroughbreds behind.

"Hey," a voice said from the doorway. "Are you accepting visitors?"

Cindy turned her head to see Christina and Melanie crowded together in the wide doorway. She smiled at the girls. "Come on in," she said, nodding at the room's single chair.

Melanie perched on the edge of the bed, and Christina sat down, a large white bag in her hands. She reached into it and produced a bouquet of bright flowers. "For you," she said, holding them up.

Cindy looked at the table beside the bed, then nodded toward the water pitcher. "I guess you can use that for a vase," she suggested. But Christina dug into the bag again and brought out a ceramic vase shaped like a rearing chestnut stallion. "We thought you'd like this, too," she said.

When Cindy saw the horse on the vase she almost started crying. The rearing stallion looked so much like Champion, he could have modeled for the artist. And now she was going to lose Champion once and for all. But she forced a cheerful face for the girls, who looked at her anxiously. "It's great," she said, feigning enthusiasm. "You can fill it at the bathroom sink."

Christina left to fill the vase and arrange the flowers, and Melanie gave Cindy a hard look. "Are you all right?" she asked in a soft voice.

Cindy shook her head sadly. "No," she said. "I'm hurt, and we won't be racing Gratis in the Derby, and we're going to lose Champion. I'm not all right at all."

Melanie nodded. "And it must be hard being stuck in a hospital bed," she said sympathetically. "I know. After my accident they kept me in the hospital overnight. I cried almost the whole time. It was awful."

Her words made Cindy feel less alone. She reached out and gave Melanie's hand a squeeze. "I'll be fine," she said. "I'm just feeling a little sorry for myself, that's all."

"Which is totally understandable," Melanie said. "When I thought I wouldn't be able to race Image in the Derby after I wrecked the Blazer, that was the worst feeling in the world. I'm so sorry, Cindy."

Christina returned with the flowers and set them on

the table. "When do you get to go home?" Christina asked, moving a couple of the bright flower buds around to balance the floral arrangement.

"Tomorrow," Cindy said. "Which is a day longer than I want to be here." She pointed at the bandage on her head. "I feel fine, but the doctor wants to keep me under observation for a while."

"We'll come by and see you once you're back home," Melanie promised, slipping off the bed.

"Thanks for coming by," Cindy said, feeling relieved when the girls left. It was hard enough being in the hospital. Trying to put on a cheerful facade took more energy than she had left.

The next morning when Ben came to get her, the nurse insisted that Cindy ride out to the car in a wheelchair. "But it's my arm that's hurt, not my legs," she protested.

"Hospital rules," the gray-haired nurse said in a no-nonsense voice.

Rather than argue, Cindy let the nurse wheel her from the room and out to the waiting pickup. Ben helped her into the cab, and they drove home in silence. When he pulled up in front of the cottage, Cindy was touched by the big Welcome Home banner strung in the doorway.

Ben eyed the sign. "From Elizabeth and Beckie, I'd say," he commented. He helped Cindy from the truck and carried her small bag and the vase of flowers to the house. "I asked them to tidy the place up for you, and Beckie said she would fix some food and leave it in the refrigerator."

"That was thoughtful," Cindy commented. "I just hope she didn't leave me any of those Vegemite sandwiches she's always eating." The Australian groom had a special fondness for the odd-tasting spread her family sent her from home, but Cindy hadn't been able to develop a taste for it.

Ben laughed. "That yeasty stuff does have a rather unique flavor, but no, I can assure you Beckie was making chicken salad when I left here."

Inside, the main room was spotless, the carpet vacuumed and the windows washed and sparkling. She raised her eyebrows. "I should hire one of those two as a housekeeper," she said, sitting down on the sofa. She felt exhausted, even though she'd only walked a few steps into the house.

"Is there anything I can get for you?" Ben asked, giving her a concerned look.

Cindy shook her head. "I have everything I need," she said, glancing at her arm, strapped securely to her side. "Except two good arms."

Ben gave her a tight-lipped smile. "If you *do* want anything, just pick up the phone," he said.

"Thank you, Ben." When he left the cottage, Cindy swung her feet up and stretched out on the sofa, trying to get comfortable with her arm's bulky wrap. She had just started to doze off when a knock at the door disturbed her.

"Now what?" she grumbled, carefully getting to her feet. When she swung the door open, Wolf was standing in the doorway, an uncertain look on his face.

Cindy looked at him for a moment, unsure what to say. Finally she gestured for him to come into the cottage and shut the door behind him. Wolf looked around the little living room, his attention settling on the display of Thoroughbred figurines. He walked to the table and stared at them for several seconds, then glanced back at Cindy. She stood in the middle of the room, feeling confused.

"I knew you were going to get into trouble with Gratis yesterday," he finally said, folding his arms across his chest.

Cindy sat down on the sofa and stared across the room at him. "You knew, huh?" His tone annoyed her just as much as ever, but she fought to keep her sharp comments to herself. She owed Wolf for saving Gratis, and her.

Wolf nodded. "I know that colt better than anyone," he told her. "I was getting my stuff out of the tack room when I saw you ride off, and I didn't want anything to happen to him, so I decided I'd better follow you."

Cindy pinched her mouth shut. At least that explained how Wolf had caught up with Gratis so quickly. "So I guess you saved Gratis," she said. "I suppose you want your job back now."

Wolf shook his head. "No. I don't want to be an exercise rider," he said decisively. "I want to be a jockey."

"But you don't have the experience yet," Cindy said.

"How am I supposed to get it if I can't get on the track?" Wolf demanded. "I need a chance to prove myself."

Cindy gazed at him for a minute. "I guess you think I could help you get your apprentice license?"

"It's the least you could do," Wolf said. "Just give me a chance to test."

Cindy took a deep breath, considering his words. "Fine," she said. "I'll set it up."

"Thanks," Wolf said, and strode across the room toward the door.

Before he opened it, Cindy cleared her throat. "Uh, Wolf?" she said. When he turned to look at her, she gave him a thin smile. "Thank you for what you did yesterday . . . really."

Wolf gave a nonchalant shrug. "I'm a good rider," he said. "It really wasn't a big deal at all. Give me a call when you have the test set up. I'd like to get it done as soon as possible."

He stepped outside and pulled the door closed behind him, leaving Cindy fuming again. How could he be so arrogant? *Fine*, she told herself, picking up the phone. She'd schedule his test. He was right—it was the least she could do for him. But did he have to be so obnoxious about asking?

In a few minutes she had set up a test at Churchill Downs, and Christina and Melanie had agreed to ride out of the gate with Wolf. He would be using Sassy Jazz, one of Whitebrook's experienced racehorses, as his mount.

Two days later, her arm still bound in its unwieldy wraps, Cindy stood beside the track at Churchill Downs, her attention on the starting gate. Christina was astride Rascal, a chestnut three-year-old colt owned by Whitebrook Farms, and Melanie was sitting on Catwink, another of Whitebrook's three-year-olds. The gray filly danced in the chute, impatient to get out and run.

Sassy, a veteran of several races, stood alert and still, her ears pricked, waiting for the cue to burst onto the track when the gate banged open.

Cindy caught herself gripping the track rail with her good hand, surprised to find herself rooting for Wolf. She didn't care one bit for his big attitude and rude comments, but still, it was exciting to test in the

149

hope of getting the track officials' approval to start racing.

She could remember her own test well: the nervous tension she had felt while waiting to ride out of the gate, the fear that she might fail, and the elation that had blazed through her when she was approved for a conditional license.

In contrast, Wolf looked relaxed and sure of himself, and Cindy wondered whether he really was that confident or whether it was a show for the girls waiting on either side of him in the starting gate.

In a moment the gate handler signaled, and the three riders crouched over their horses' withers, prepared for the moment the gate would open. When it did, the three horses surged onto the track and galloped along the straight stretch. Wolf rode well, handling Sassy easily between the two younger horses. After they had galloped almost four furlongs, Christina and Melanie slowed their mounts, and Wolf did the same, circling Sassy around to return to the gate. Cindy could see his confident expression waver a little as he rode up to the group of track officials who had been overseeing the test.

In a minute she saw his fist shoot into the air, and his excited "All *right!*" echoed across the field. She caught herself smiling, knowing how wonderful it felt to be okayed by the grim-faced men who could deny a license as easily as they could approve one.

Wolf leaped from Sassy's back and led the mare to where Cindy waited at the rail. His beaming face made her feel good about her decision to give him the chance to test.

"That was so great!" he exclaimed when he reached her. "I can hardly wait to ride in a real race."

Cindy nodded, smiling. "Maybe we can schedule you this week," she said. "I'll see if I can find a horse for you to ride."

"Do you mean it?" Wolf asked, his eyes growing brighter.

Cindy nodded. "You've earned a shot at racing," she admitted grudgingly.

For a moment Wolf's expression turned serious. Then a smile lit his face. "Thanks a lot, Cindy," he said sincerely. "I really appreciate your giving me this chance." He patted Sassy's sleek black nose. "I'll go take care of my horse now."

As he walked away, Cindy acknowledged that Wolf might be an irritating pain in the neck, but he seemed to be really grateful for the chance she'd given him. For the first time since she'd been told she could no longer race, Cindy felt the ache she carried in her heart fade a little.

She turned away from the track and gazed at the grandstand. So she couldn't race anymore. She could accept that now, and do her best to be one of the top trainers in the country. And even if she would never get to feel the excitement of coming out of the starting gate again, she'd found something else that made her feel almost as good. She'd been able to help another up-and-coming jockey get a chance to race, and she was sure there would be other young riders she could help. To her amazement, it made her feel better than she had in a long time.

12

"Can you come up to the house?" Ben asked Cindy. He stood in the office doorway, dressed in a polo shirt and tan slacks, looking every bit the wealthy Thoroughbred stable owner he was.

Cindy smiled up at Ben, the warm feeling she had gotten after helping Wolf still with her. "Sure," she said. "Do you need me right now?"

Ben gave her a curious look, then nodded. "We're expecting a visitor, and I want you there," he said. He continued to stare at her, and Cindy frowned at him.

"What?" she finally asked.

"You look even more radiant than you did the day

153

we brought Champion home," he said, smiling. "You seem different somehow."

Cindy wrinkled her nose at him. "I'm the same old Cindy," she said. "You know, stubborn, headstrong." She pointed at her bandaged arm and rolled her eyes. "And impulsive." She couldn't explain to him how helping Wolf had affected her. She didn't know if it would make sense to anyone but herself.

"I need to get up to the house," Ben said. "Our visitor will be here shortly."

"I'll be there," Cindy said absently as he walked away, still absorbing what Ben had told her. She and Wolf, alike? She shook her head in amazement. As hard as it was to admit, she realized Ben was right. She cringed inwardly. That was probably the main reason she and Wolf had such a conflict. He wasn't much different from how she had been at his age, full of confidence and dismayed that the rest of the world never saw her the way she saw herself. She sank back against her chair and sighed. "That's kind of embarrassing," she muttered to herself.

Finally she tidied the stacks of paper on her desk and left the office, walking briskly up the long drive to the mansion. She let herself in and crossed the spacious entry, pausing in Ben's office doorway. He sat at his desk, intently reading through a stack of papers.

Cindy knocked lightly on the doorjamb, and he looked up, waving her into the room. "Have a seat," he said. He rose and crossed the room to where a coffee service was set up. He poured a cup of coffee and added sugar and cream, then gave it to Cindy. "Just the way you like it, right?" he asked as she took a sip.

"Perfect," she replied. "Thank you. But, Ben, you know I can't stand suspense. Tell me what's going on."

Ben returned to the other side of his desk and smiled broadly. "You'll see in a few minutes," he said, sounding more cheerful than he had in several days.

Cindy leaned back in her chair and enjoyed her coffee, taking the time to gaze around the large office. She spent a minute admiring the artwork that had been hung around the room, her attention settling on a painting that looked remarkably like Champion with the Arabian desert in the background. She rose to take a closer look at the picture and realized it was a perfectly rendered painting of the stallion when he was much younger.

Ben glanced up and looked toward the painting.

"That was a piece my father commissioned not long after you left Dubai," he said. "I was thinking you might like to have it at the cottage."

Cindy felt her smile fade a little. It wouldn't be long before Champion was gone. The painting might be the only thing she would have to remind herself of him. "I'd love it," she said softly.

A loud knock sounded at the door, and Ben leaned back in his chair, waiting. Cindy turned to see the housekeeper cross the foyer to answer the door. In a moment Brad strode into the office, looking furious.

Cindy felt her stomach tighten, and she gripped her coffee cup tightly, staying silent.

"What did you call me over here for?" Brad demanded angrily, glaring across the desk at Ben. "The message said you had some vital information regarding Wonder's Champion."

Cindy went rigid, looking from Ben to Brad.

Ben held up a piece of paper, forcing Brad to lean over the desk to take it. Ben glanced at Cindy and winked, and she felt a thrill of excitement. Ben's calm confidence could mean only one thing: He must have found out something about Champion's ownership.

She cocked her head to see Brad's expression, which was turning darker by the minute.

"I forgot to tell you," Ben said, looking at Cindy with a twinkle in his eye. "My father is doing quite well. He called me as soon as he got home from the hospital." Ben's smile broadened as he glanced at Brad.

"Feel free to take those documents to your attorney and have them checked out any way you like," Ben said. "The sale of Wonder's Champion to the al-Rihani stables was quite legal and quite properly done." He nodded toward the door. "Our business is done now, and I believe it's time for you to leave."

With an irate grunt, Brad spun on his heel and stormed from the office. Cindy could hear the hard slapping of his soles against the tile of the foyer as he strode to the door, and she bit her lower lip as Brad slammed the door shut behind him. A moment later the engine of his sports car roared to life, and, unable to contain herself, Cindy burst into laughter as they heard him speed down the drive.

Her eyes met Ben's, and they gazed at each other across the desk. "You did save Champion," Cindy said, shaking her head.

Ben grinned as he rose from his chair and came around the desk, holding out additional copies of the documents to Cindy. "My father was outraged," he said. "He faxed all the paperwork he could find to keep Brad from trying to cheat us out of our Triple Crown winner."

Cindy took the papers and smiled up at Ben. "I'll put these in the office files," she said. "We don't want any more questions about ownership on any of our horses."

"That's a good idea," Ben said.

Without thinking about what she was doing, Cindy threw her arm around Ben's neck and gave him a kiss on the cheek. "Thank you so much," she said.

When she stepped back, Ben's smile was even wider. "See?" he said. "You're impulsive. I like that."

Cindy felt herself blush a little, and she ducked her head. "Me and Wolf," she said, laughing at herself.

Ben raised his eyebrows. "I must say, if young Wolf tried to hug and kiss me like that, I don't think I'd like it nearly as well." He gazed at Cindy for a minute. "Have you settled on a race to let him use his new license?"

Cindy nodded. "I think we're going to let Gratis run

one more race before the Derby," she said. "It isn't as though he's been run to exhaustion by racing every couple of weeks. It'll be more like giving him a good breeze."

Ben nodded. "That's a wise decision," he said. "I'm looking forward to seeing our colt on the track."

"Me too," Cindy said. "Me too."

Before she returned to her office at the barn, Cindy walked with Ben out to Champion's pasture. The stallion raised his head when he saw his visitors, and with a low nicker he crossed the field to meet them at the fence.

Cindy reached up to rub Champion's glistening neck. "You really and truly are safe at home now, fellow," she said.

"He's going to stay right here," Ben agreed. "No one can take him away from us." He pointed at the papers Cindy still held. "When you read through those, you'll find that my father signed ownership of Champion over to us."

"You mean over to Tall Oaks," Cindy corrected him.

He shook his head. "No," he said. "Look at the documents. Wonder's Champion is now owned by Ben al-Rihani and Cindy McLean, equal shares."

Cindy stared at Ben, unable to believe what she was hearing. Half ownership in Champion? "You can't be serious," she said. "Your father couldn't have done that."

Ben nodded. "I told you before—my father is as stubborn and mulish as you are, Cindy. But over the years he has mellowed. He, too, followed your career when you raced in New York. He may not be able to say it to your face, but my father respects and admires you. Giving you a half interest in your beloved Champion is the best way he can tell you he is sorry for his mistakes."

Cindy felt as if she had slipped into a dream. "Pinch me," she said to Ben. "None of this seems real."

"It's very real," Ben said, giving her arm a tiny squeeze. "And right now I see Wolf heading this way. He looks quite serious. I guess you need to go take care of business, and I, too, have work to do."

Cindy turned to face Wolf as Ben headed back up to the house. Wolf had an anxious look on his face as he approached. He had an envelope in his hand, and he held it out to her. "I got my license today," he said, not sounding very happy.

Cindy took the card he offered her and glanced at it, then looked back at Wolf. "It looks like every other jockey's license I've ever seen," she said, then bit back a smile. "Your name is really Wolfgang Wiedemann? I thought Wolf was something you came up with yourself."

Wolf glared at her. "Why would I do that?" he asked. "It's just that nobody calls me by my full name."

Cindy shrugged. "I guess they will now," she said.

"I guess," Wolf replied, taking the license back.

"Are you ready for tomorrow?" Cindy asked.

Wolf's face brightened. "You bet," he said. "Gratis and I are going to scare the other horses right off the track at Churchill Downs. I can hardly wait to win the race."

Cindy worked her jaw for a second, then shook her head. "Don't assume you'll be sitting pretty in the winner's circle after your first race," she warned him. "It always takes a few races to get a feel for the competition." She sighed. One thing was certain—Wolf was never going to be hampered by a lack of self-confidence.

Wolf grinned at her. "I know I'll be on the best horse on the track," he said confidently. "You'd better get dressed up tomorrow so you look good for the photographers."

Feeling her annoyance build, Cindy exhaled heavily. "Just be sure you have everything ready so we can trailer up there first thing in the morning," she told Wolf.

"I will," he promised, then turned back toward the barn. Cindy watched him stride away, his confident strut making her waver between irritation and amusement. She followed him to the barn and went into the office to get her own work done.

When they arrived at the track during the predawn hours the next day, Wolf was unusually quiet.

"Are you nervous?" Ben asked him as Cindy opened the trailer door. When Wolf led Gratis out of the trailer, the colt had his head high and his tail flagged, and he was snorting excitedly. His head snapped back and forth as he took in the activity around the track's backside.

Wolf looked from the energetic colt to Ben and gave a half smile. "No way," he said, patting Gratis's sleek neck.

But Cindy could hear the edge in his voice, and she smiled to herself. "Being a little nervous isn't a bad thing," she informed Wolf. "It'll keep you alert."

Beckie, the young groom, had come along to be Gratis's handler for the race, and she stood to the side, looking wide-eyed around the track. "This is so exciting," she said. "Shall we take Gratis over to the receiving barn?"

"You and Wolf can do that," Cindy said. She grinned to herself at the way Beckie looked at Wolf. Just what he needed—an adoring fan to feed his ego.

But Wolf smiled back at Beckie with genuine warmth. "I guess we'd better head over there," he said. They led Gratis away, leaving Ben and Cindy to explore the backside, checking out the rest of the day's competition.

As they strolled along the shed rows, looking at the horses, Ben glanced at Cindy. "Do you think there's a little romance brewing between our two employees?" he asked, sounding amused.

"It sure looks that way," Cindy said. "Maybe some of Beckie's sweet personality will rub off on Wolf." *And maybe some of Ben's levelheadedness and patience will rub off on me*, she added to herself.

Ben laughed. "We'll have to wait and see," he said.

By the time the day's races had begun, both Wolf and Gratis had settled down a little. A few minutes before Wolf was scheduled to race, Cindy joined Ben in the viewing paddock, standing at the number six spot. She looked around at the other owners and released a contented sigh.

"I never thought I'd be standing here with the owners," she said.

"Welcome to the big time," Ben said, smiling down at her. "You do look quite the part of the refined Thoroughbred owner, by the way."

Cindy glanced down at herself. She still wore the sling, but, dressed in beige slacks and a green silk blouse, she looked like a successful owner and trainer on race day—at least a little bit. "Here they come," she said, pointing toward the shed where Beckie had brought Gratis to be saddled. Wolf walked into the viewing paddock and stood beside Ben. He swept his hands down the green-and-purple silk shirt he wore and tugged at the waistband of his nylon breeches.

"Do those silks fit all right?" Cindy asked, watching his nervous gestures.

Wolf nodded. "They're great," he said. "I just can't believe I'm wearing them."

"You'll be fine," Cindy told him as Beckie brought

164

Gratis around the paddock. She saw a familiar group at the paddock rail and waved to Mike and Ashleigh. Beside them Ian and Beth, Cindy's adoptive parents, were smiling proudly. Ian waved and gave Cindy a thumbs-up, causing Cindy's wide smile to grow even brighter.

"I'm really here as an owner," she said, a sense of amazement filling her as the reality finally hit home.

Melanie and Christina stood at the rail with Cindy's sister, Samantha, and her husband, Tor, beside them.

Beckie stopped Gratis in front of them, and Ben stepped forward to give Wolf a leg up onto Gratis's tall back.

"Good luck," Cindy said.

Wolf grinned down at her, his confidence returning as he adjusted his stirrups and collected his reins. Cindy had a sudden memory of herself doing the same things, feeling a surge of sureness as she settled onto a familiar racehorse's back.

"I don't need luck," Wolf said. "I've got Gratis." Beckie led them to the waiting pony rider, while Cindy and Ben joined their friends and family to gather at the track rail and watch the post parade.

After a short warm-up gallop, the horses were

loaded into the starting gate. Cindy waited anxiously for the starting bell, her eyes locked on the distant gate, tension radiating through her. She gripped the rail with both hands, and when she felt a warm pressure covering her hand, she glanced down to see Ben give her a comforting squeeze.

"They'll be fine," he reassured her, and Cindy darted him a weak smile.

"I know," she said. "It's just so different watching it all from this perspective. I've never had my own horse racing before."

"Get used to it," Ben said, leaving his hand over hers.

When the gate snapped open, Cindy felt as though an electric shock had hit her. She went rigid, her eyes locked on the bay colt in the number six position.

"Look at Wolf go!" Christina exclaimed, leaning over the rail. "No one is going to be able to touch them!"

Cindy blinked in amazement as she watched Wolf skillfully negotiate the crush of horses. Within seconds he had moved Gratis to the rail, avoiding the tightly packed horses and getting the colt to the front of the field.

At six furlongs Wolf and Gratis were still in the lead.

The three-quarter-mile race would be over quickly, Cindy knew. Still, she felt anxious, afraid Wolf would push Gratis too hard. But Wolf shot a quick glance under his arm to see where the rest of the horses were, then rated the colt. He held his position at the front of the pack but kept Gratis's pace slow enough that the colt had plenty of fire when they came around the curve and headed toward the finish line.

A gray colt suddenly put on a burst of speed, moving up quickly to challenge Gratis's lead. Cindy held her breath as the gray came up beside Gratis. The two horses ran nose to nose for a few seconds. Cindy was certain Wolf would fall back into second place. But Wolf balanced himself over the colt's shoulders and Gratis sped up, nosing ahead of the gray as they closed in on the finish line. She felt Ben's hand tighten on hers. In tense silence they watched the end of the race.

"Go, go, go!" Melanie and Christina screamed beside her. "Pick it up, Wolf!"

Cindy realized she was still holding her breath, and as Gratis crossed the line a nose ahead of the gray, she released it with a loud whoosh.

"We won!" she exclaimed, turning to give Ben an

elated hug. She looked back to see Wolf circle Gratis around. He rode the prancing colt to the winner's circle, a huge smile splitting his face. Beckie slipped onto the track and caught Gratis's headstall so that Wolf could dismount. Cindy watched the groom fling her arms around Wolf, giving him a quick hug. From where she stood, Cindy could see Wolf's face go pink, but his grin stretched from ear to ear.

"Ben!" Cindy said, gripping Ben's arm as the reality hit her. "He really won the race!"

"Time to head for the winner's circle," Ashleigh reminded her, giving Cindy a gentle push in the right direction.

When they met Wolf at the winner's circle, the young jockey was laughing and joking with the clerk of the scales as he weighed in, his racing saddle slung over his arm. Cindy stood near Gratis, rubbing the sweating colt's nose gently while they waited for Wolf to remount the horse and pose for the photos and brief ceremony.

When he returned from the scale, he grinned at Cindy. "I guess you'll be wanting me to race him in the Derby, right?"

Cindy stared at him in shock, unable to believe his nerve.

"Maybe we can squeeze in a few races on some other horses between now and then," Ben spoke up, giving Wolf a stern look. "If you prove yourself consistently, Ms. McLean and I could discuss your racing Gratis for us in May."

Wolf looked wide-eyed from Cindy to Ben, then puffed his chest out. "Bring them on!" he said. "I'll have you spending so much time in the winner's circle, you'll think it's home."

Cindy gave a soft snort, but after seeing Wolf's skill that afternoon in winning his first race, she was starting to think he might be right.

"Why not?" she said boldly. "We'll get you in some other races to give you a little more experience, but it looks to me like you're Gratis's only hope."

Wolf's eyes widened. His shocked look made Cindy realize that he'd never expected her to make the offer, even though he'd been insisting all along that he was meant to be Gratis's jockey.

"You know I'd do a great job for you," he promised sincerely.

"I believe you will," Cindy said. Ben gave her hand a quick squeeze, and when she looked up at him, he gave her a warm smile of approval.

Cindy caught sight of a familiar face near the rail. When she focused in that direction, she saw Brad Townsend, scowling. She offered him a cheerful wave and a smile, but Brad curled his lip angrily and turned away, shoving through the crowd toward the backside.

"There's not a thing he can do to us now," Ben said to Cindy as they watched Brad storm away.

"No, I think we're free of Brad's interference," she agreed. "What a relief."

She looked back up at Ben, and a sense of happiness she'd never experienced before coursed through her. She smiled at the handsome man, who lowered his head and pressed a light kiss to her lips. A sudden flash made Cindy realize that one of the track photographers had caught the moment, and she froze, her lips touching Ben's, a smile tugging at her mouth. Just when she'd thought she had nothing left to hope for, everything was finally going right. As they left the winner's circle, she realized that even though she couldn't race, she still had a bright future ahead of her.

MARY NEWHALL ANDERSON spent her childhood exploring back roads and trails on horseback with her best friend. She now lives with her husband, her horse-crazy daughter, Danielle, and five horses on Washington State's Olympic Peninsula. Mary has published novels and short stories for both adults and young adults.